Daisy's Summer Mission

Daisy's Summer Mission

Hannah Pearl

Stories that inspire emotions!
www.rubyfiction.com

Copyright © 2021 Hannah Pearl

Published 2021 by Ruby Fiction
Penrose House, Crawley Drive, Camberley, Surrey GU15 2AB, UK
www.rubyfiction.com

The right of Hannah Pearl to be identified as the Author of this Work has been asserted by her in accordance with the Copyright, Designs and Patents Act 1988

All characters and events in this publication, other than those clearly in the public domain, are fictitious and any resemblance to actual persons, living or dead, is purely coincidental

All rights reserved. No part of this publication may be reproduced, stored in a retrieval system, or transmitted in any form or by any means, electronic, mechanical, photocopying, recording or otherwise, without the prior permission of the publisher or a licence permitting restricted copying. In the UK such licences are issued by the Copyright Licensing Agency, Barnards Inn, 86 Fetter Lane, London EC4A 1EN

A CIP catalogue record for this book is available from the British Library

ISBN: 978-1-91255-053-1

Printed and bound in Great Britain by Clays Ltd, Elcograf S.p.A.

In loving memory of Uncle Stuart.

Acknowledgements

The final stages of this book were written whilst we were all on lockdown because of Covid 19, and so foremost in my mind is my gratitude to the scores of people who are out on the front line, keeping us safe, keeping us fed, keeping us going.

I'm grateful to the amazing staff of the NHS, scientists, shop workers, delivery people, Royal Mail staff, refuse collectors, teachers, people pulling together in their communities to help their friends and neighbours.

It makes the scary news a little less scary.

It helps the world feel smaller.

It helps the isolated feel just a little less alone.

Thank you.

A thanks also to the Tasting Panel readers who passed the manuscript for *Daisy's Summer Mission* and made publication possible especially to Mel Russell, Jo Osborne, Sharon Walsh, Carol Fletcher, Vanessa Wick and Gill Leivers.

Chapter One

A breeze lifted the cotton of my shirt and tickled my skin, bringing to mind the breath of a hot lover trailing kisses down my back. The sun was fierce, every inhalation brought heat so thick that I could feel it filling my lungs like syrup. Beads of condensation ran down the outside of my glass and dripped onto the rickety wooden table next to my sun lounger. I took a sip, tasted fruit and vodka, crunched an ice cube and felt it soothe me. Sighing with pleasure, I set the drink down, lifted the shirt over my head and dropped it onto the floor. I laid on my front and closed my eyes. Bliss. Reaching behind me, I untied the string on my bikini top. Within moments I heard a splash coming from the outdoor pool and felt a shadow block the sun's glorious rays.

'You'll burn,' said a quiet voice to my left. 'Let me take care of you.' A cap snapped open and closed on a bottle. I braced, ready for the cool liquid to touch my skin, but instead Eli rubbed the lotion between his hands to warm it. I groaned with pleasure from the first touch, and he paused before running his hands from my neck to the small of my back. He took his time to ensure that my skin was thoroughly protected, and it was a sweet, sweet torture. I knew what his fingers were capable of when we were alone.

'I like these strings,' Eli said, letting his fingers skim millimetres below the fabric of my bikini bottoms before gliding up again. He rubbed more cream onto my shoulders, massaging it in.

'You're right, I'd better be careful not to burn. Maybe we should go inside for a little while?' My voice sounded husky even to my own ears. My boyfriend grinned. He loved knowing how my body reacted to his touch.

'I could do with getting out of these wet shorts,' Eli said, his voice dipping dangerously.

I sat up, only just remembering to hold my bikini top up before I flashed the rest of the guests around the pool. Eli took my other hand and together we ran for the villa. It was barely ten yards – we had paid extra to have rooms so close to the pool – and yet it still felt too far suddenly.

Behind us I heard my best friend, Lily, talking to my brother. 'Where are they off to in such a hurry?'

'Daisy doesn't want to burn, and Eli wants to take his trunks off,' Ben told her. I didn't need to turn around to imagine how big Lily's grin would be. 'Why are you smiling?' Ben asked her. 'They're only going to their room.'

I loved how unaware my brother was at times, but it didn't stop me suggesting to Eli that next time we took a trip, we ought to come alone.

'It wasn't my fault,' he protested, as he dug into his pockets to find the key to our room. 'When I mentioned that I'd booked a week in Greece I hadn't expected Ben to assume that I had booked for him too.'

'You did take him on the last trip. And my dad.' I rested my hand on his back. We were both as desperate as each other to get back inside.

'I guess we were lucky that there were so many of us that we got a group discount this time.' He didn't sound happy though. Having to ensure that we spent time with everyone that we had brought with us had put a damper on how we had planned to occupy ourselves. Eli nearly hadn't bothered to bring any trunks at all as he had hoped not to leave our bedroom except for food.

'Hopefully between Cody stopping to take photographs every few steps and your dad popping in to every bakery he sees, they should be out for a while. There are a few things I've been hoping to do on holiday too.' He pushed the door open and I rushed in behind him.

I locked the door behind us. After that I didn't speak again, apart from to tell Eli how much I was enjoying his attention. Afterwards, I rested my head on his bare chest, our breathing in synch as we waited for our pulse rates to drop back down to normal again.

'I love you,' I told him, feeling him pause for a moment beneath me. Now he was breathing in as I breathed out. 'I'm going to tell you until you get used to hearing it. And until you believe me,' I said.

'I do believe you,' he replied. He ought to. I'd loved him for a decade, and bickered with him throughout it, until we had teamed up last Christmas to find my missing brother and finally allowed our feelings to surface. We had been so used to trying to protect Ben that we hadn't seen how much he had grown up or just how capable he was. Ben had fallen in love, and when Eli and I had fought, Ben had run off to find Erin.

I was desperate to get Ben home safely before my dad returned from his trip and discovered that it had been mine and Eli's behaviour that had caused Ben to leave. I'd never had forgiven myself if my actions had put my brother at risk, especially when I was so used to looking out for him. Eli had felt the same, and it had forced us to work together to try and find him. Under pressure, we'd no longer been able to deny how we felt about each other. It had been a terrifying experience, but I was grateful that it had brought us together. I needed him, but he needed me just as much.

'I love you,' I said again, making eye contact as I spoke. The curtains fluttered, and I pulled the sheet up to cover us. It was growing darker outside now, and we hadn't stopped to switch a light on before we had tumbled into bed, but I could see Eli's eyes despite the gloom, narrowed and serious, as he looked back at me.

'I feel the same way, Daisy. I just don't find it as easy to say as you do. I haven't exactly been in touch with my feelings the last few years.' He was referring to the time since his mum had passed away, leaving him without any other family.

'I loved you then too.'

'I could tell.' He snorted. 'It was obvious from the way that you glared at me.'

'Only because you usually had a dolly bird hanging off your arm.'

'If I had known you were jealous ...' he began.

'It wouldn't have made any difference. You'd have been too scared of upsetting Ben.' My brother had known that when I fell in love I would be all in and he had feared that Eli, despite being his best friend, wasn't necessarily capable of doing the same. We'd had a brief 'moment' when we were teenagers, but Eli had allowed his fear to hold him back from seeing where it might have led. I hadn't. And I'd been all in ever since, even if it had taken an epic road trip and the fear of losing Ben to bring us back together again. This time I was determined not to let Eli go so easily.

'Speaking of which, I promised we could go out for burgers tonight. Ben wasn't too sure about the feta in the salad at lunchtime.' Eli got out of bed. I took the chance to sneak a peek at his backside. 'Are you coming too?'

'In a minute,' I told him, 'I'm just enjoying the view.'

He laughed as he pulled his jeans up and zipped the fly. He crossed back to the bed and leaned over me. 'I do love you, Daisy,' he said, dropping a lazy kiss on my lips. 'Now, let's get a move on before Lily chooses where we eat. I don't want to get served by a bunch of topless men again. How does Taylor put up with her?'

'She means well,' I pointed out. 'Lily just has a healthy appetite. For food, I mean.'

He laughed again and tossed me my shirt. 'Come on. I'm sure even Ben has worked out what we've been doing by now. And I can't tell you how strange it feels to face your dad when we've spent the afternoon in bed together.'

'Not as weird as yesterday when he and Cody disappeared to buy a round of drinks and didn't get back for an hour. His T-shirt was on back to front afterwards.' I shuddered.

'You should be proud of him,' Eli joked. 'Isn't it nice to know that you can get lucky even at his age?'

'Careful or I'll tell him you said that.'

'You wouldn't dare.'

I reached for my sarong. 'Who's going to stop me?' Eli reached for me and lifted me back onto the bed, tickling me until I squealed. It was fully dark before we finally left the room.

The poolside was empty, but for a pair of honeymooners holding hands over a wire table which had grown rusty in the sea air. Their bottle of sparkling wine sat ignored, growing flatter and warmer as they kissed. Pots of palm trees ringed the outside of the square. Dad, Cody, Ben and Lily were nowhere to be seen. I checked my mobile. 'No texts. You?'

Eli checked his own. 'Nothing. Hang on though.' He tapped a few buttons, opened a map app and glancing around us, pointed up an olive-tree-lined path towards the hills. 'Ben is that way.'

'Does he know that you can track his mobile?'

Eli raised one eyebrow at me. 'Do you think there's anything online that Ben doesn't know?'

The air was growing cooler now and I wished I'd had brought a cardigan with me. I shivered, and within moments Eli had stopped walking, kissed me quickly and dashed back to our room. He returned a minute later and handed me a jacket.

'What did I ever do without you?' I asked.

'You lusted after my body from a distance.'

I'd have made a clever retort, but I couldn't disagree.

Chapter Two

The following day dawned just as clear and bright. 'I needed this break,' Eli said, climbing from the pool and letting the water drip down his torso. I wanted to reply but I was too busy watching a droplet. Finally it disappeared, absorbed by his trunks, and I looked up and met his eyes. They twinkled with laughter, but I could see the lines of tiredness underneath still.

'That last assignment was a bad one?' I asked.

'Wish I could tell you. Actually, I don't. It was tough going and I was very happy to come home to you afterwards and try to forget it.' It was always this way with Eli's work. He did something mysterious for the Government and I'd never found out exactly what this entailed. Shortly before our trip he had been away for a fortnight, returning exhausted. He had lost weight, not that he had carried much spare to begin with, and it had taken several days before he had slept well. There had been one night when he had been in the throes of a nightmare and I'd had to hold him as he had tossed and turned, stroking his head and whispering to him until it had ended. In the morning he had no memory of it.

'At least they let you have a decent chunk of time off now to recover.'

'They've promised me a couple of months of being office-based. I never thought I'd be glad to hear that.'

He dived back into the pool, swimming half a length before he came up for air. I tried to imagine Eli in an office job, sat in a room from nine 'til five, working away at his desk, stopping for tea and to gossip by the water cooler. He was going to be pacing like a caged animal by lunchtime. On his first day. By the end of the rest break he'd be climbing the walls. Still, it was nice to know that the most dangerous activity he would be faced with would be taking Ben to buy the newest computer game release. Given that Ben had once come home with a nosebleed after being 'mugged' for the last remaining copy of a popular new game in the shop by a particularly vicious teenage girl, I was pleased for my brother that he would make it home unscathed next time.

Lily came and sat with me on the poolside, slipping her feet into the water next to mine. 'Having a nice time?'

'Perfect,' I told her. 'I wish it could be like this all of the time. Eli is relaxed, Dad and Cody seem happy. Where's Taylor?'

Lily's rugby playing boyfriend worked with Ben and Eli. Not that they got on well. I wondered whether it stemmed from when we first got to know him, six months earlier, and he had displayed an interest in me. We had never acted on it, and in fact it had helped spur Eli into finally admitting his feelings towards me, but there was an undercurrent of tension whenever the two of them were together. Though Eli had been snippy with him from the outset, so it was possible that there was a rivalry at work which I'd unwittingly stepped into the middle of.

'We didn't get much sleep last night.' She winked at me. 'He's gone for a nap.'

'And you didn't go with him to lie down?' I smirked.

'I did, but afterwards he fell asleep. I don't know why orgasms always make men sleepy. I've never felt so alive.' She threw her arms in the air, thrusting her bust forward. Across the pool, the honeymooners were back. The man choked on his cocktail, and his wife swatted his arm. He must have offered a string of denials or apologies because after a few minutes she finally began to return his kisses once more. Lily remained oblivious.

'Let's go on a snack run,' I suggested, standing up and heading towards my room to fetch my handbag.

'Good idea' Lily agreed. 'I think I burnt off all the calories

I ate at breakfast. So did you, judging by the smile on your face.'

Eli was right; we were definitely going on holiday alone next time. For now though I was going to enjoy the extra time with my friend. Lily and I linked arms and walked up the dusty brick path towards the village square. We passed the tavern where we had eaten the night before. Now closed, the wooden chairs were up on top of the tables, and a small woman dressed in black, complete with head scarf and white shawl around her shoulders, pushed a mop across the red floor tiles.

Lily's heels made a staccato beat on the paving slabs. My own straw espadrilles made a softer thud, and these were almost the only sounds. In a few weeks the schools would break up and the beaches surrounding us would be full of families desperate for sunshine and rest, but for now it felt as though we had the world to ourselves.

'It's nice to come for a walk with you,' Lily told me. 'I feel like we hardly get any time together any more.'

I apologised, but it was true. Between my working hours and Lily's, plus both of us being in relationships, we spent a lot less time together than we used to and I had missed her. 'Let's make the most of the trip,' I told her. 'I fancy getting something nice to eat for when we're back at the villa.'

Inside the small grocery shop I picked up a battered metal basket and began to fill it with pots of olives and fresh peaches. Lily added loaves of bread, still warm from the oven. We added bottles of mineral water from the fridge at the back of the store. As the glass door closed afterwards the motor sputtered as the machine struggled to cool itself again. I lifted a strand of hair from where it had stuck itself to my forehead and daydreamed about getting back to the pool again.

The man behind the till had several days' growth of peppered stubble on his cheeks, but he greeted us with a smile. We had fun admiring some of the crafts made for the tourists, and currently displayed only in hope that a few of us might wander this far this early in the season. Later in the year he would have the certain knowledge that hordes would soon need to find the perfect last-minute gift to take home for granny. I knew the feeling well. He chatted as he rang up our finds, and though I didn't understand a word of it, his cheerfulness was evident. Lily snagged a further addition of a bulbous bottle of local wine, now dusty as it had probably been waiting here since the last tourists left at the end of the previous summer.

I gave the shop keeper a handful of Euros. Heaving the laden cotton bags onto our shoulders, Lily and I wished the man a happy day in our very broken few words of Greek. He came out from behind the counter and gave us each a brief hug. I wasn't quite sure what we had done to deserve his affection, but Lily took it in her stride. She frequently gathered attention from people who mistook her body confidence as an invitation and so was adept at sensing when a gesture was simply friendly and how much was too much. I'd seen her leave guys twice her size huddled over in the foetal position if they crossed the line. In this case the shop keeper's affection seemed to be a gesture of gratitude that we had enjoyed visiting his business. For a moment it was enough to make me miss my own shop and my favourite clients.

Back in London I specialised in sourcing the perfect romantic gifts for loved ones. My boutique operated from the bottom floor of my dad's tall Tudor town-house in central London. The building had previously been my grandad's, and then my dad's, bakery, but had lain empty after my mum died when Ben and I were six. When I had decided to open my shop a few years earlier, we had turned the back room into my bedroom so I now lived downstairs too. I found it cosy. Eli found it cramped, but he knew I loved living there and so he kept his mouth shut and tried not to complain when he banged his head on a low ceiling or I trod on his toes when we tried to pass in the hall. However, when we had to squeeze into the bathroom to take hurried showers before work he enjoyed its charms too. He'd been late more than once recently when we'd got especially close in there.

Lily called my name, and I snapped my attention back to the present. She pointed at a small green lizard that was sunning itself on the pavement. 'Let's go and bake ourselves a bit more too. If our summer at home is as wet as last year's, this might be our only chance to get a tan.'

We tore chunks from the loaf and munched on the bread as we walked. 'Are you having a nice time with Taylor?' I asked.

Lily nodded and grinned. 'He's very sporty so he has a lot of stamina, if you know what I mean.' She added such a huge wink I'd have had to be daft to miss her point. 'And he's a nice guy. He puts a lot of energy into making sure I'm taken care of.' I didn't look to see if Lily winked after that too.

'Does this mean that you might be tempted to try …' I dropped my voice to a whisper, 'monogamy?'

'Steady on,' she cautioned, reaching her hand down into the front of her vest top and making sure that her girls were front and centre. If the guy on his honeymoon had been watching her he'd have fared a lot worse than just choking on his drink. And he'd probably spend the night sleeping alone outside on a bench. 'I didn't say that I was hanging up my handcuffs just yet. But if I were, he'd be worth it.' I swapped all the bags to my right arm so that I could stretch across with my left and pull my friend in for a hug. I wasn't tall, maybe five-foot-six in my sandals, but the top of Lily's head came to just under my chin.

'And you? All good now that you finally bagged Eli?'

'All good,' I assured her.

Lily had had some reservations. It wasn't surprising. She had spent hours in the past hearing me bang on about what a serial flirt Eli was with anyone in a skirt. She had listened to me rant about how smug he was, and how annoying. Now that we were together, she had to listen to me talk about how gorgeous and thoughtful he was, and whenever he was away she got to put up with me moping and missing him. To her credit though, she had never once asked whether I was sure. Instead, she had been happy for me and had gone out of her way this trip to make sure that we had time together, sending my Dad or Ben on errands or outings. Now she hurried to keep up with me as I marched ahead, keen to get back to the rest of the gang. I was pleased that my dad and brother were happier and more confident than they had ever been but, having had to look after them for so long, it was tough to let go.

We got back to the pool in time to watch Eli and Taylor dive in. They were sleek and powerful underwater, and when they surfaced to breathe, I heard Lily gasp and found myself doing the same, as we enjoyed watching them power their way down the pool. Taylor was taller and broader, but Eli's muscles were tight and lean. And I think he wanted it more. As they neared the end of the pool, Eli edged ahead, touching the wall a split second before Taylor.

They both climbed out, panting, their chests heaving with effort, as they turned to face us. 'Who won?' Eli asked.

Lily and I looked at each other and spoke in unison. 'Draw. It was a draw.'

Taylor clapped Eli on the back. It might have been just a tad hard, as Eli looked like he had to stop himself from toppling over, but he accepted our verdict with good grace and came over to raid the food. Taylor and Lily disappeared off back to their room with a pot of something chocolatey and gooey that Lily had picked up from our new friend in the shop.

'I was sure I beat him at the end there,' Eli said, snuggling me against his wet body and nibbling my ear. My T-shirt grew soaked as it absorbed the water from his body. It would have been a very nice way to cool down if I hadn't felt my body growing hot in all sorts of ways as soon as he was close.

'You would have been insufferable if you had won. We'd never have heard the end of it.'

'He really wanted to beat me. Maybe he's still jealous that I won you.'

'I'll remind you that I'm my own person, not a prize at the fair.' I poked his bare chest. He grinned and I leaned into him again. 'But yeah, you got me. I don't think Taylor minds though. He's probably getting up to things in there that we can't even dream of.'

'Oh? I've got a few ideas of my own,' Eli said, scooping me up and carrying me into our villa. Slamming the door behind him, he laid me on the bed and made sure that he had my full attention.

I woke up later and treated myself to a shower as Eli napped. The dreams seemed to have ended and he looked more relaxed than he had since his return. He hadn't put on all the weight that he had lost though, which reminded me that Lily and I had left our bag of shopping outside in the sun several hours ago. I threw on a yellow dress with embroidered white flowers which I hoped accentuated my mousy brown hair as well as being my namesake flower. Slipping my feet into a pair of white flip-flops I let myself out. The bag was still where I'd left it next to the pool so I picked it up and began to look through to see what could be salvaged.

Ben was sat at a table with his mobile phone. 'What are you up to?' I asked him.

'My friend was supposed to ring me this morning. I didn't hear from her. Or him. I was just trying to get online to see if I can find her. Or him.' His vague attempt at subterfuge didn't fool me for a second. Ben wasn't skilled at deception. He'd never seen the point before.

'You mean Erin, don't you?' I said. He didn't answer. 'Given that everyone else you know is here, you must mean Erin.'

Ben still didn't confirm that I was right, though I knew I was. He and Erin had met at work and got together but he hadn't told us. He worried that we wouldn't think he was capable of an adult relationship and that we would interfere. He had been right. And wrong. Ben's relationship with Erin had become complicated during our adventures the year before. When Ben reached out to Erin, after he ran away from me and Eli, she'd been angry at Eli for not being aware of Ben's dislike for his womanising, and angry at me for my overprotectiveness. She had wanted to give Ben the opportunity to grow without us overshadowing him. I'd have valued her opinions a great deal more if she hadn't doped my twin brother up and sneaked him on to a ferry to give him that space. Eli, Lily, Taylor and I had rescued him, only to end up with him and Erin both angry at us.

I'd been in favour of reporting Erin to the police, but Eli and Taylor had pointed out that doing so might risk Ben's security clearance, and without that he would lose his job. Ben was the smartest man I'd ever met; he could fix anything electronic, programme any computer, he sometimes saw the world in a very different way to me, but he had a huge heart. He had accepted that Erin should have behaved better, but he wasn't angry with her. I was. To my great reluctance, we had agreed not to report Erin, and in return she had agreed to undertake a course of counselling. Recently she had been to visit my dad to explain that she was sorry for giving Ben a sedative and taking him on the boat. Dad had mellowed on the issue of her and Ben seeing each other. I had not. I saw my behaviour as protective. Ben saw it as holding a grudge.

We had agreed not to fight about it on holiday, but I was finding it hard to keep my mouth shut.

'I just wanted to say hello to her,' Ben said, kicking the chair opposite him. Its legs grated as they scraped across the flagstones, letting loose a screech that hurt my ears. I acted as if he had been hinting for me to sit down and took the chair.

A door closed behind me, and a moment later Eli joined us at the table. I handed him the bottle of red wine from the shopping trip earlier. He took a Swiss army knife from his pocket and fiddled with it until he found the corkscrew attachment. I reached back in the bag and found a packet of plastic cups that we'd also found in the shop. Eli poured. The bread had gone a little hard in the meantime, but it still smelled amazing so I tore a chunk off and began to chew.

'To us,' Eli said, raising his cup. I lifted mine to tap against his. It lacked the satisfying clink of a proper glass, but the fruitiness of the liquid washed my bread down perfectly. Ben lifted his too, albeit without the enthusiasm. Taylor and Lily came to join us, and I passed them each a cup of wine.

'What's the plan for dinner?' Lily asked.

'Dad's been chatting with the people in the taverna. They've been swapping recipes this afternoon. He said if we get there for eight-ish we can try some of his cooking,' Ben said. I was used to Ben not making eye contact as he spoke, but even for him, he looked subdued. He finished his wine and handed me the empty cup without looking up once.

'Are you coming with us?' I asked him.

He shrugged. 'Might as well.'

I looked at Eli. He shook his head. There wasn't much we could do. Either Ben got over how much he cared about Erin, or we got used to the idea that he was dating someone who had tricked him. At present, neither option seemed likely.

'Let's go and eat,' Taylor said. Eli must have overcome

some of his earlier objections to Taylor, as he accepted the suggestion without any of the smart remarks he'd have made in the past. Or maybe he was just as hungry as I was given that we had been too busy to eat a proper lunch. Either way, he held his hand out for me to hold as we walked. It had taken him a while to get used to doing that too and I appreciated the gesture.

Dad had recently begun to emerge from a twenty-year fog of grief and widowhood and was making the most of his second chance at life. He and Cody, a photographer who had set up a shop opposite mine six months earlier, had recently begun dating. Dad had swapped his slippers and cardigans for tie-dyed T-shirts and a denim jacket. Cody greeted us at the door to the taverna. She was wearing a flowing cream linen dress. It was less colourful than her usual garb, but as she had long auburn hair tied up in a purple silk scarf, the effect was still eye-catching. I hugged her warmly, grateful for the joy that she brought to my dad.

'There's salad and bread on the table, wine in the jug. Phil is just putting the final dishes in the oven, then he and Christos are going to join us and tell us all about their creations,' Cody announced. I couldn't get used to hearing my dad referred to by his name, and not just as 'Dad', but thinking back to the doddery old man he had been before he met her, I was thrilled. I reached across and hugged her again.

The door to the taverna opened, and when I looked past her to see who had come in, I nearly dropped my glass.

Chapter Three

'Erin,' I hissed. Ben jumped up and went to hug her. He kissed her cheek and she beamed at him. Eli rested a hand on my arm to stop me from getting up and asking her to leave. Because that was all I was thinking of doing to her. Nothing violent at all. Honestly.

'How did you find us?' Ben asked.

'Do you think she tracks his phone too?' I whispered to Eli.

'You sent me details about the villa. When I got there it was almost deserted, but there was a couple who pointed me in the direction of the village.'

Dad chose that moment to burst through the three-quarter height shutter doors. 'Who's hungry?' He set a terracotta dish covered in melted cheese on the table. 'This one is vegetarian,' he told Cody and me.

The owner followed him out carrying plates of thinly sliced cured meats. He set these on the table next to a jug of olive oil. He began passing out small plates, but when he noticed us all staring at Erin and not talking, he set the rest on the table and scarpered back to the kitchen.

Dad, ever the gentleman, guided Erin to a seat and poured her a drink. 'I'm just going to fetch the last dish.' He turned to me and Eli. 'Be nice until I get back.' It was a command, not a suggestion.

I crossed my arms and sat back in my seat. Ben fussed around Erin, stroking her hand and telling her about his holiday. He'd made a deal with the villa owners to build them a new website in return for access to their personal wi-fi password. It was much faster than the guest system that the rest of us were on. As a result, he'd had a project to keep him busy and enough broadband to keep him from complaining.

'I'm glad to see you,' Ben said, and I noted that he did manage to look at Erin as he spoke.

'Me too,' she told him. 'There are some messages for Eli and Taylor from work. I offered to come and deliver them.'

'We have phones,' I told her.

'Do they have secure lines?' Ben scoffed.

I shrugged. 'Email?'

'Do you know how insecure that is?'

I did. I remembered only too well finding Ben reading my emails once as a teenager. He said he had been looking for an idea for a birthday present for me. I'd given him a smart clip round the ear and he hadn't done it again. Thankfully he had also either not noticed how many of my messages were about Eli, or they hadn't been relevant to his search and he had simply ignored them. I could never have been so disciplined.

'You shouldn't write anything in an email that you wouldn't write on the back of a postcard,' Erin said, picking up her wine and taking a sip. Ben looked at her proudly. She clearly listened when he talked online security. She continued, 'You know, recently we got a new email system at work. Supposed to be secure. Encrypted. Unbreakable. Within half an hour we'd received an email from the Boss telling us that we were all getting the afternoon off, just because.'

We all turned to look at Ben. 'No-one could prove who sent it,' he said, blushing. Anyone could tell he looked guilty, and he worked with a bunch of super spies. I couldn't imagine that he had fooled his colleagues, but apparently he had.

Erin took a sip of her wine and continued. 'The Boss was in the middle of a meeting with her counterpart from France. She came back out to a half empty office. None of the people she was supposed to introduce him to were there. You could practically see the smoke coming from her nostrils.'

'Should have let me design it in the first place.' Ben pouted.

'How do you not get fired?' I asked him.

'I wanted to point out that if it could be hacked that quickly, then imagine the dangers if anything important had been sent with it.' It made sense, in a Ben kind of a way, but it highlighted how differently Ben's brain worked sometimes.

'You could have just told them,' Erin pointed out, and to give her some credit, she said it much more gently than I would have. I could only imagine how their Boss had reacted.

My brother didn't seem to mind her trying to guide his actions as much as he did when I tried. I wondered whether she was any more successful than I had been but soon got my answer. He took over telling the next piece of the story. 'We went back to our previous system, but I had a couple of hours free and the new system was sat there not doing anything. The office was half empty so I had time to play.' My heart began to hammer at the thought of what Ben might have got up to. 'I added some fake historical data, made up a bunch of emails. Maybe made sure that the new addresses got accidentally leaked to some unsavoury contacts,' Ben continued.

'He set up a sting,' Erin chipped in. 'Our French colleague came back the following morning for the rearranged meetings. Ben decided to join in. Halfway through he got bored, stood up and announced that if they really wanted to make an impact, they ought to get teams in place to catch the gang about to break into a warehouse in the French countryside. He'd created information suggesting that it was a stockpile of explosive materials and decommissioned weapons, forgotten and barely guarded. Boss lady choked on her coffee, went red in the face and looked like she was about to collapse.'

'And I got called in to smooth it over,' Eli continued. 'That's where I was on my last trip. We had a couple of hours' notice to rig this warehouse up, and sure enough, the next morning we arrested a group of would-be terrorists. We caught four people, red handed, carrying enough weapons to put them away for the rest of their natural lives and then some.'

Erin piped up again. 'Not to mention that one of them had been wanted in connection with a previous terrorist incident. He was one of the most wanted suspects in France. Ben now has an all-expenses paid trip to Paris waiting for him, anytime he can get there. He'd have official honours but they don't like to publicise our department if they can help it.' She kissed his cheek. Ben preened under her attention.

'You didn't want to give them a bit more time to get their plans in order?' I asked him.

'You're not still annoyed that you'd made dinner and I had to leave for the mission without eating it?' Eli asked me. I didn't reply because I *was* still cross. The dinner had taken me ages, and I'd even got Lily to hook me up with some new knickers that I'd hoped to show him afterwards. They'd had so many laces and strings that it had taken me longer to put them on than to make the food.

'So, Ben isn't in trouble at work?' I asked.

'Well, they were pleased when he asked for some time off for this holiday. I think they were all ready for a quiet recovery spell, but no, they know how lucky they are to have him.' Erin stroked Ben's cheek and he snuggled into her. I wanted to puke.

'That still doesn't explain why you're here,' I said. I realised I sounded snotty, and usually I tried really hard to be nice to people, but she had kidnapped my brother. I decided that I was entitled to still be a bit snippy with her.

Eli and Taylor made eye contact, and there was none of the snarling that usually accompanied it. Ben was oblivious. He and Erin were far too busy mooning at each other. He had his arms around her waist now, and she was sweeping the hair from his eyes, taking measure of how he looked, as if she could tell from his face whether he'd been eating well or sleeping enough. Finally, she seemed to have taken enough of an inventory and she turned to face us again. 'Do you mind if we eat first? The sandwiches on the plane weren't very appetising. I'll tell you more once we get back to the villa.'

Dad busied himself making sure that we all had full plates. Now that he had rediscovered his love of cooking he couldn't abide the thought of anyone going hungry. I knew that Erin was biding her time to try to talk to Eli, Ben and Taylor in private, but Dad had worked so hard to prepare the food, I bit my tongue. I figured that being quiet was at least better than being openly rude. I felt proud of myself for making that concession. Besides, it was difficult to make small talk whilst waiting to find out if there were issues of national security at risk, and even more so if they meant that Eli would be called away again before he got all of the recovery time he needed. Thank goodness Cody was there, and she bustled around making sure that we all had several glasses of local wine, showed us her photographs and talked about her plans for a day trip to some ruins the next day. I had soon thawed and was able to join the conversation again.

Eventually we had eaten all the food, Dad paid the bill and we walked en masse back to our villas. Dad and Cody bade us goodnight before retiring to their room. Seeing them walking off holding hands was just the heart warmer I needed as I waited to find out why Erin had travelled all the way out here just to pass on some news. Whatever it was, it wouldn't be good. Eli and Taylor hung around the front door to Ben's place, and it became evident that they were waiting for Lily and I to leave before they went in to talk.

'I just need to pee,' Lily said. She hustled past them and ducked inside before I could make my customary comments about not needing to know every detail. She was back within moments and grabbed my arm, dragging me away as she wished the others a good evening.

Pulling me behind her, she darted around to the back of the villa where a small window broke up the expanse of white-washed stones. 'I opened it when I went to the loo. Maybe we can hear what they're talking about.'

My natural nosiness battled with the knowledge that I shouldn't be getting involved. 'Should we be listening? They keep these things secret for a reason,' I pointed out, but I was already trying to work out how we could get close enough to hear. The window was about six feet high. 'How did you reach to open it in the first place?'

'Stood on the side of the bath.' Lily shrugged. 'Come on, give me a boost up.'

She lifted her foot and began to try and dig it into my hip to get a step up. Grunting with effort, I linked my hands together and tried to heave her up. Lily wasn't big. Height-wise I was taller, but she was much more curvaceous than me. Enough to cause drivers to mount pavements when she walked past. Enough that I couldn't take her weight for as long as she evidently needed.

'I don't think I can hold on,' I warned her, wobbling and trying to move my feet to gain better traction.

'Move left, just a bit. I can hold on to the window-sill. Don't let go. I can't reach …' Her stiletto caught me in the gut, and I folded, letting go of her legs as I tried to catch my breath. 'Daisy, I'm going to … Ahhh!'

Chapter Four

'I knew I heard something. What were you two up to?' Eli helped lift Lily off me, and once her bounteous cleavage had cleared my head I could breathe again.

'They were trying to listen in,' Taylor said. Eli handed Lily to him and reached out to help pull me up. I smoothed my skirt back down to cover my knickers and could tell Eli was annoyed when he didn't watch.

'It was Lily's idea,' I huffed.

'You might as well come inside so that we can continue,' Erin added. I hadn't seen her come around the corner, and though I didn't want our admittance to be at her say so, I wanted to know what was going on. 'I think we can trust you and we need to talk. This can't wait until we get back to the office.'

We trooped back inside. Ben was sat on the small sofa to the left of the door, and Erin stood next to him, their fingers linked. Taylor sat next to Ben, and Lily sat on his knee. Eli paced the room, leaving no obvious spot for me. With all the chairs taken, I crossed to the far wall, sat down and waited for someone to explain what was going on.

'The Boss set a bunch of us on clean-up tasks after you left.' Eli didn't respond as Erin continued to explain. I tried to get him to look at me, but he wouldn't.

'At least I understand now why you came home so tired, running around on Ben's missions,' I said to him. He still didn't reply.

Erin continued as if I hadn't spoken. 'Then she told us she was taking a few days off to unwind. Told us she'd be back soon, but it's been longer than we'd expected and we can't reach her. She's not answering her phone or email. She never stays out of touch for this long. Even when she had surgery last year they kicked me out after she called me in to the recovery bay to take notes for her. I tried to reach her boss, but they won't tell us a thing. The office is unsettled, and no-one knows what to do. With you all here, most of the senior team are away. I just want to check in with her. In our line of work, we like to know our people are okay, not assume they are, just in case. And that's pretty much where we had got to when we heard you outside.'

'Trying to listen to the confidential discussion in here,' Eli pointed out.

Ben opened his laptop and began to type. 'Are you searching for her or setting up another terrorist bust?' I asked. He ignored me. As did Eli. Lily laughed, but only briefly. With everyone else looking so serious perhaps it wasn't the time to try and lighten the mood with a joke just yet.

'Got her,' Ben said a moment later. I was shocked. When I'd tried to search online to find out who Cody was when she first moved to London I'd got nowhere. Similarly, when Ben had gone missing it had taken us days of searching, hundreds of miles of driving and a whole lot of luck to find him.

'I thought you'd switched back to the more secure online system?' I asked.

'We did,' Ben responded.

'Let me get this straight, no-one in your office, with all of your spyware and resources, could find the Boss but it took Ben less than a minute?' I scoffed. Ben looked hurt. 'I do realise of course, dear brother, that you are unusually skilled.' That mollified him at least.

'She's worked in that office for thirty years. You don't last that long without learning a few skills to help you evade people,' Erin said.

'So, where is she?' Eli asked, drawing our attention back to the important topic at hand.

'Somewhere called "The Getaway Centre",' Ben said, reading from his screen.

Lily snapped her fingers, making me jump. 'I've heard of that.'

'I doubt it,' Ben said, turning his laptop around so that we could all see the screen. 'It's barely got any online presence. The only references I can find are buried several layers deep under the name of a holding company.'

'How do you know she's really there?' Taylor asked. The rest of us just stared at him. If Ben said she was, then that was good enough for us.

Ben shifted in his seat and stared at his shoes. Obviously it wasn't just from her phone records or an email. 'I know I'm not supposed to look at medical records,' he began. I was relieved that Eli and I had finally taught him that. 'But I checked everything else that I could and there was no sign. She gets private health insurance through work which covers mental health care. She needs it because of the level of security which she works at. She's so good about making sure we take breaks when we need them to keep ourselves well that I wondered whether she was taking some time for herself. She was pretty cross with me when I left.' It must have been bad for Ben to have noticed, unless Erin had explained it to him. Even I had to admit that it was a useful skill that she could unravel social interactions for my brother.

Ben and Eli had access to this insurance too. Eli didn't use the option to talk to doctors or therapists. He barely talked to me about how he felt after work, but I was hoping that the longer we were together the more he would open up.

'Her doctor mentioned that she had been under a great deal of stress at work.' Ben flushed as he spoke, and I wondered if he was aware of how much of this had probably been due to his behaviour or whether it was because he knew he shouldn't have found that out. 'There is a note that she suggested our Boss took a break and go to a rehab centre for some mental health time.'

Erin let out a huge sigh of relief. Taylor lifted Lily off his lap and disappeared, quickly returning with a bottle of ouzo and a stack of cups. He poured and began to pass them around.

Erin took a timid sip of hers. I wondered if she was nervous of the drink or of all of us watching her. 'They'll be very pleased to know nothing nefarious was behind her absence.' I wanted to point out the utter hypocrisy that she had put us through the same worry when she had taken Ben away. 'I'll just send a text and let the office know that we've found her,' Erin added.

'I thought texts weren't secure?' I asked. 'Isn't that why you had to come all of this way. Surely if you could just have texted we wouldn't have needed to go to all of this trouble?'

Eli shot me a look and I realised that maybe I had gone too far. Luckily Erin ignored my moodiness and answered my question anyway. 'I couldn't have put her name in a text just in case, but now I can just write back and say "got her". They'll know what I mean. Thank goodness Ben is such a genius.' She stroked his face and he beamed at her.

'Why didn't she tell you that she had booked herself a trip?' I asked. It seemed that an awful lot of stress could have been avoided if she had. Especially my stress at having Erin appear in my holiday.

'Maybe it was a last-minute decision. It was a very tense week,' Taylor said. Ben looked uncomfortable and Erin squeezed his hand for reassurance.

'Maybe she just wanted a little bit of privacy,' Ben suggested, as though it hadn't been him who had breached it to discover her whereabouts.

'Talking about mental health and needing time out isn't exactly easy,' I added. It certainly wasn't for Eli. 'But now we know maybe we can all go back to whatever we were doing before.' As in, Erin could go home again. Hopefully.

'She probably thought we could manage without her,' Erin admitted. 'The deputy manager they hired to try and take some pressure off her isn't working quite as well as we'd hoped. He doesn't quite have the ...'

'... Backbone that she does?' Taylor suggested.

'Gravitas,' Erin supplied, rather more tactfully. 'He should have put an end to the whispering straight away. He probably thought he was giving her a break, but he didn't realise that in a business like ours, people worry when someone who is usually so steadfast disappears. But now we know she's safe, I'll pass on the news and we can put a stop to all of the rumours.'

'I think it's time we left,' Eli said. Taylor and Lily bade us all a goodnight and walked out. I stayed, lingering over my drink. 'You're supposed to down it like a shot,' Eli pointed out.

I knocked it back but still didn't make a move to stand up. Eli took my hand and pulled me gently to my feet. 'We need to talk,' he said. His fingers on my wrist were gentle. I could have pulled my arm clear if I'd wanted to and he wouldn't have stopped me, but the strength in his voice kept me in his thrall and I did as he wished.

He stopped at the door just long enough to carry out a protracted and overly complicated handshake with Ben, before leading the way to our own villa. The name was a little misleading; the 'villa' was in reality only a bedroom, bathroom and sitting room, with a small two-seat sofa. It had a small counter at the back wall, set along the top of the fridge, which held a kettle, a bowl of ripe peaches, and that was all.

Eli closed the door behind me and I flinched, waiting for him to raise his voice as he let me know, in no uncertain terms, what he thought I'd done wrong. He stayed silent however, making for the fridge where he fetched two bottles of ice-cold lager. He uncapped the lid of the first and offered it to me. Tense with the pressure of waiting for him to explain, I took it and drank half in my first swallow. The bubbles shot up my nose, making it sting and my eyes water. I set the bottle on the counter and tried to rub the ache away with my fingertips.

'Always classy,' Eli commented, and I was relieved to see that he was smiling, albeit only with the corner of his beautiful mouth, just where I loved to drop a kiss. He uncapped his own drink and took a swig, managing to look as cool and suave as ever.

I wanted to stick my tongue out at him, and indeed until recently this would have been my reaction, but these days I valued his opinions and truly wanted to make peace. 'I'm sorry about what happened outside,' I began.

'Because you were caught, or because you shouldn't have been trying to listen?'

'Lily wanted to know what you were up to.'

'And I'm sure you took a great deal of persuasion to help her.' He wandered through to our room where he set his drink down next to the bed and began to unbutton his shirt.

'It's only because I care about you,' I tried. 'You come home so tense when you go away for work. I just wanted to understand why.'

'Dammit, I don't want you to know,' he snapped, dropping his head down into his hands. 'For goodness sake, Daisy. It's bad enough that I have to go on these missions. Can't you just leave it?' His voice now was louder and tighter than I'd heard it in a long time.

'I'm sorry,' I said, setting my own drink down and sitting behind him on the bed. I began to massage his shoulders, and slowly I felt the tension begin to slip away.

'Don't you get it?' he said. 'You're cheerful, and optimistic and so full of goodness. I don't want you to know what my work is like because I want to come home to you and be reminded of how much joy you bring people. It helps me to forget what evil is out there, and it makes me determined to protect you, and our country.'

He fell silent after that, and I reached around from behind him to fasten my arms around his waist. 'I get that. I don't agree though. I don't think I need protecting. You're my partner, so if you're experiencing something, however awful it is, I want to know. As much as I'm allowed at least. And I will always support you. It's not going to change me, I will always believe in the inherent goodness of people, but I will respect how you feel and not try to eavesdrop on your work again.'

'I want to keep you safe. I need to keep you safe. I can't lose you, Daisy.'

'You won't, but you can't keep me wrapped up in cotton wool either.'

'I know. I hate feeling like I'm trying to control you. It's not that I want to stop you being yourself ...'

'You can't keep me safe just by keeping me in the dark. I worry about you. I know there will be details you can't tell me because of the level of security involved, but I hate feeling like you never tell me anything at all.' My voice rose as I tried to explain myself. I didn't want it to, I wasn't cross with Eli. I could understand his fears, but I hated that he thought it was okay to risk himself but that I was somehow too vulnerable or too weak to know.

He took my hand and pulled me into him for a hug. He kissed the top of my head and I could feel us both relax as we let go of the tension and remembered that what was actually important was just being together. 'I will tell you what I can,' he promised.

'And I'll ask you when I want to know something. I won't go behind your back again.'

'And Lily?'

'I make no promises for Lily,' I said, raising my hands in defeat. He turned to face me, and I was relieved to see that he was smiling again. 'Lily doesn't like to be told what to do, but you can try if you feel brave enough.'

Eli shook his head. 'I'd rather face down an armed terrorist.'

Chapter Five

Despite Ben's success at tracking down the location of their Boss, we all felt more subdued on the journey home. Lily was finally sleeping off all the sexercise she and Taylor had indulged in. Ben was holding tight to Erin's hand. She probably thought he was being romantic. I was trying to work out whether he was a nervous flyer or fighting to keep himself calm due to having no access to any electronic communications for three hours. Eli and Taylor occasionally traded a few hushed words, which was unusual enough that I noticed every time they did it. I suspected that as soon as we got home they would be disappearing off to the office to help hold the fort until their Boss returned. Cody fussed over my dad. He had a touch of sunburn on his nose, and he in turn was raving about some photographs that she had taken that he wanted to print and frame for his living room.

I had scored the window seat and spent most of the journey watching the sunshine fall away behind us. I didn't mind that we were going home. I loved my shop and had sourced some little treasures, wrapped in my suitcase, for a few favourite clients. It had been lovely to spend so much time with Eli, though with so many people around us it hadn't been as romantic as I'd hoped. Perhaps it was knowing that when we got home real life would intervene again. We could never predict when or for how long Eli would be called away. Until recently I'd always tried to talk myself into believing he was somewhere safe, but that was wishful thinking. I'd had enough loss in my life, with my mum passing away when Ben and I were kids. How would I cope if anything happened to Eli now that we had finally accepted our feelings for each other? On holiday, it had felt as though we'd reached an understanding about his job, and that he was slowly beginning to let me in to his world. Now we had to see how that held up once we were back in our old routines.

I pulled a cardigan from my rucksack and wrapped it around my shoulders as if it were a blanket. Turning my face back to the window, I tucked my feet up on my seat and curled myself into a ball, feeling a little tearful at the knowledge that real life could get in the way again very soon. I stayed that way until Eli tapped me on the shoulder.

'Did you want some tea?'

I blinked to make sure that he couldn't see the moisture in my eyes before I faced him. 'Please,' I said, reaching into my bag to find some cash. He rested his hand on mine and used the other to hand some Euros to the stewardess.

'Two please.'

'Three, actually,' Lily said, adding her order.

'I wouldn't mind a cup as well,' my dad said. Eli handed over the last of his Euros, refusing to let anyone else chip in. Perhaps he suspected, as I did, that whatever had sent his Boss running for a break would end up being his problem to deal with sooner or later and he wanted to get one final treat in whilst he could.

'Penny for your thoughts?' Eli asked as he handed me a scalding hot paper cup.

'I didn't think you'd have any pennies left after paying for the drinks,' I told him, trying to lighten my mood with a bad joke. He must have guessed what I was up to because he didn't push, just handed me a packet of shortbread biscuits and a small pot of long-life milk.

We didn't speak again until the plane approached the runway. The light was fading, and the landing strip was lit up against the dusk. I swallowed to relieve the pressure in my ears and Eli reached to take my hand. His were still, unlike mine which were both shaky and more than a little clammy. I tried to wipe them quickly on my dress first but they were still sticky. He didn't seem to mind though he must have been able to feel it. 'Don't you ever get scared?' I asked as the plane bumped and jolted before finally resting all its wheels on the ground and beginning to brake.

'No, I trust the pilots. They land these things all the time.' I didn't bother to reply to him. The silence stretched out until he finally spoke again. 'Sometimes,' he admitted. 'When we end up going off on one of your brother's last-minute set-ups and we've had less time than I would like to prepare. Most of the tasks we go to are pretty routine, but every now and then we'll get something a little more serious. But it's how you use that fear. I like to think that it keeps me sharp. Stops me getting sloppy and making mistakes.'

I gave his hand a squeeze but didn't have time to ask any more. We'd reached the terminal and the doors were about to open. I was happy to wait for everyone else to disembark first but Ben had other ideas. 'Too many people,' he moaned, and I was glad for once that Erin was there to soothe him instead of me or Eli having to do it. He'd never enjoyed being in big crowds, and I was relieved that Eli had booked a taxi to take us all home so that we didn't have to face the underground as well.

'My car is parked over there,' Erin said, pointing off into the distance as we finally made it to the front door of the airport after being reunited with our suitcases. The temperature here was far cooler than we had enjoyed on holiday and I was glad of my cardigan. Dad, however, looked chilly.

'Great, don't let us keep you. Have a safe drive,' I said, smiling briefly, even if it didn't reach my eyes. I began to walk to the taxi pick-up point.

'See you tomorrow,' Ben called, and it took me a minute to realise that he was talking to us and not Erin.

'Ben ...' I began, but Dad waved to stop me.

'Let him go, Daisy. We need to give him some space one day.'

'If she hurts him ...' I began.

'She won't,' Dad assured me. I wasn't sure I could be as certain as he was, but he was right to remind me to step back. Ben had been angry with me that I'd found it hard to accept that he didn't need as much protecting any more. I had to give him some space now to find out for himself whether his relationship was a healthy one. But if Erin did mess him around, none of them would be able to stop me from going after her.

Back home Lily and Taylor bid us goodnight and disappeared off into the dark to do whatever it was they did. Probably best not to ask. Dad followed Cody back to her's, saying something about seeing her photos from the trip. If he had the need to reminisce about the holiday so quickly I wasn't going to stop him, and if there was another reason for them to go off together then I didn't want to know.

At my front door I paused to see whether Eli was going to come in with me or return to his own place. He was fussing over the bags in the boot, so I headed in to my flat and left the door open to see whether he followed me. The candles and bath salts that lined one wall of my shop lent a lingering scent of lavender and rose. It was good to be home. I wondered if Eli felt the same about his place. He spent so much time with me or Ben that I'd barely ever been to his flat. It had been small and sparsely decorated last time I saw it. I'd itched to make it more cosy with a few photos and personal touches, but as Eli tended to use it mostly for storage, staying only long enough to pack fresh clothes, he'd never bothered to add any.

Switching the light on inside my flat, I scooped a pile of junk mail and bills from the doormat and dropped them onto the glass counter which displayed some of my more expensive merchandise. Eli followed me in and closed the door. I breathed a sigh of relief, realising how much I had wanted him to stay.

'I'll take a shower, then I'll go and get some fresh bread and milk for breakfast,' I told him.

'Why don't we both take a shower and I'll buy coffee on the way into work tomorrow?'

I liked Eli's suggestion even better. I slept well, feeling safe and cherished in his arms. The morning came all too quickly.

'Will you be home tonight?' Eli asked, kissing me as he reached for a T-shirt.

I nodded. 'I've only got one client due in today so I might close up for a while and catch up on laundry.' I swallowed. 'Do you have any more clothes in your bag? Save you going home for a clean shirt before you head in for work? I can think of something we could do if we had an extra half an hour.'

Eli kissed me again. 'I've only got my holiday gear in there. I won't get away with going in to the office in my trunks. Only Ben could do that without getting fired.'

I nodded. I understood, but even after a week with him I still didn't want to let him go. Plus, now I was daydreaming about how good he had looked in the pool again. He snapped me out of it by speaking again. 'How about I grab a bag and come here after? I could get back for seven-ish?'

Thankfully I didn't have much time to miss him. Arthur arrived just as Eli turned the corner and was lost from sight. I showed him into the shop and left him investigating the pottery and scarves that I had brought back with me.

'Are you sure you're alright, sweetheart?' he asked after I'd shown him the same vase for the third time.

I smiled at him. 'Would you be alright here for ten minutes whilst I nip to the shop? I'm going to buy some fresh bread and milk then I'll fix us a cuppa and some toast, and we can find something perfect for your wife's birthday.'

That was one of the things I loved most about my job. My favourite customers were also my friends, and Arthur could be relied on to tell me heart-warming stories about his wife and their family which would leave me glowing inside long after he left. Arthur had been married for fifty years to his best friend, and he never failed to inspire me when he visited. My parents had loved each other but I'd been so little when my mum had passed away, so I hadn't been aware at that age just how special their love for each other was. I learnt a lot from my customers instead.

'Respect,' Arthur told me, after I got back and was handing him a mug. 'That's the secret to a strong relationship. We love each other, obviously, but we also treat each other with a lot of respect. We talk, but we also listen. We don't do things that we know would upset each other on purpose, try never to be thoughtless. Not saying we're perfect, mind you. We're only human after all. We make mistakes, me more than the Mrs if I'm honest. But when we do, we make peace, and we forgive. You won't get far if you hold a grudge.'

I handed him the packet of biscuits that I'd bought. 'That's good advice,' I said. 'I'll make sure that when Eli gets home I'm not cross any more that he left me all his dirty pants to wash.'

Arthur laughed. 'And I hope that your young man has the sense to apologise. It cost me a huge bunch of flowers when I did that once.'

Chapter Six

'That's a big overnight bag.'

Eli dropped an enormous black holdall on the floor next to my bed. 'Thought it might save me going home for a few days. Do you mind? I should have asked if you had room.'

He had a point. My living space wasn't exactly spacious. My bedroom was crowded with treasures that I had found on my shopping expeditions and hadn't been able to bring myself to part with. There was the huge trunk next to my bed in lieu of a bedside table with a green glass hurricane lamp on top. I had a small chest of drawers, the surface hidden under an assortment of beautiful old-fashioned scent bottles and silver pill and trinket boxes. Admitting that I had perhaps kept more of them than I needed, I gathered an armful and carried them through to my shop, leaving them on the counter to polish and price up the next day.

I came back in to find Eli still looking around to find a place to put his bag. I wasn't slovenly, but I wasn't as tidy as Ben, and since I had moved downstairs I had taken the opportunity to spread. I dashed about, picking up the handful of clothes from the floor and throwing them into my wicker laundry basket in the corner. My shoes were quickly straightened and set in pairs next to the door.

'That's better.' The floor was clear and there was enough space to walk from one side of the room to the other.

Eli glanced at his bag, then back at me. He cleared his throat. Eli was never at a loss for words. I waited. Prompting him would only leave him feeling cornered. I gave him space and finally he filled it.

'I was thinking maybe I could unpack, maybe leave some things here on a more long-term basis?'

He might not have been expecting me to fling myself at

him and throw my arms around his neck, but he caught me nonetheless, and once more I admired the strength of his biceps. 'I'd like that,' I told him. We'd waited such a long time to get together, I didn't want to lose another decade now before we got more serious.

'Did you leave anything at your flat?' I asked him. It was a pretty enormous bag that he'd brought.

'Not much,' he admitted.

I kissed him again. 'Now that we're roommates, kind of, I think we should celebrate.' So we did.

Waking up in the morning was bliss, snuggling against his bare skin, knowing that he didn't have to leave to go home and change before work. We had time for a leisurely shower and a coffee, and I kissed him goodbye with just a few minutes to go until my shop was due to open. He'd unpacked only as much as he had needed to have clean clothes for work. I planned to have some more space cleared and ready for him when he got home.

Summer days were often quiet. Peak times for business for me were Christmas and the run-up to Valentine's Day. I had a slow but steady stream of customers throughout the rest of the year, with a scattering of birthdays and anniversaries, but walk-in trade was vastly reduced. After putting a bag of my old clothes aside to take to a charity shop and managing to empty a drawer for Eli's use, I took the time to give the shop a quick spring clean. I dusted and wiped fingerprints from the bulbous silver candlestick holders on a shelf. For some reason they were especially tactile and many a customer was drawn to pick them up. I didn't mind that no-one had bought them yet. If they ever found a home, I'd miss them.

I boxed up receipts ready to deliver to my accountant and ordered a new supply of the silk underwear sets that sold well during the heat of summer. Looking at my watch, I realised that it was barely ten o'clock and I was bored. I texted Lily, assuming that she would still be asleep and would find the message when she woke up. I jumped when my phone beeped to alert me to her reply within the minute.

Lily could score a few hours off work too. A shopping expedition was just what I needed. Packing a sun hat so I didn't burn and fetching a leather notebook which contained details of my long-standing clients' preferences and special dates, I was soon ready.

Lily was waiting at the station when I got there. 'What's the plan?' she asked.

I waved my book at her. 'Time to start stocking up. There's a couple of antique stalls at Greenwich Market that I want to look at, and there's a handful of items in an auction this afternoon if they don't go for crazy money.'

'Have we got time for pie and mash?' Lily asked.

'Always,' I told her, and she took my arm as we walked. Lily had paired her tiny denim shorts with red velvet platform shoes that had heels at least four inches high. I wore a long black cotton skirt, a pale blue blouse tied at my waist cow-girl style and flat black sandals. Lily therefore looked to be only a couple of inches shorter than me, not that anyone noticed. Next to her I might as well have been invisible. When we first started to hang out I found it amusing, and occasionally, if I was having a particularly bad spell of lusting after Eli, I found it upsetting. Lily never set out to steal attention though – she'd never do that to the sisterhood – but she had an energy, a vibrancy, which drew people to her. Besides, she had once offered to make me over to help me gain attention too, but at the sight of the meagre scraps of fabric that she had offered to dress me in, I had chickened out. Now that I was secure in my relationship with Eli, I didn't mind fading into the background again. It was lovely to watch Lily being herself.

She greeted stall holders as though they were long-lost friends, flirted shamelessly to score a bargain, laughing all the time to show that she was only playing. We walked away, carting shopping bags heaving with carved statues, glass sculptures and beautiful purses. We'd made it a hundred yards down the road before the stall holder caught up to us. I paused for a moment, adding up the totals in my head to make sure that I hadn't been undercharged in case he was asking for more cash, but instead he handed Lily an origami rose that he had folded from pages torn from his magazine. She blew him a kiss but refused his requests for a telephone number.

'Taylor must be something special,' I commented. 'In days past, a man that cute wouldn't have needed to ask for your telephone number.'

'I'd have dragged him into his van and got to know him better. What can I say? Taylor is growing on me.'

'I hope he doesn't grow any more. He's huge already.'

'Why do you think I'm not looking around at the moment?' Lily said, winking at me. I groaned. 'Seriously though, he's a nice guy. We have fun. But enough about my experiment with monogamy. How are you and Eli getting on?'

'He moved a bag in last night,' I told Lily, squealing with excitement. 'Sometimes I have to pinch myself to believe that it's real. I liked him for so long.'

'I know, and I was only there for the last few years of your mooning over him,' Lily teased.

'It does feel like we wasted a lot of time that we could have been together.'

'If he wasn't ready then it wouldn't have happened anyway,' Lily said.

'How did you get so wise about relationships when you haven't had many yourself?' I asked her.

'Oh, I had relationships, they just didn't take very long.'

By the time we made it home, it was teatime, though the sun still shone. I let myself into my flat, dropping the bags behind the counter to sort the following day, and called out 'honey, I'm home!' There was no answer.

Chapter Seven

The scent of bacon wafted down the stairs from my dad's flat. Even though I'd been vegetarian for years, the smell still made my mouth water. I knew that Eli would have been powerless to resist and so I followed my nose upstairs and found him in the kitchen with Ben, Erin and my dad.

Dad was stood at the stove flipping sheets of perfectly fried bacon onto the dish. Ben was cutting perfectly straight slices of Dad's homemade bread and Erin was buttering them. Eli was sat at the table, his long legs stretched out underneath. He wore a charcoal-grey suit, black shirt and a tie, which he had loosened but not removed completely. My mouth began to water and it had nothing to do with the scent of dinner. He saw me, stood up and dropped a gentle kiss on my lips, then crossed to the fridge. Removing a pack of halloumi, he handed it to my dad.

Without another word, Dad removed a second frying pan and began to assemble a sandwich for me. Eli handed me the ketchup and I added a liberal amount to my dinner. Taking a huge bite, I groaned with pleasure. Eli's eyes flashed. I sensed him tensing up and recalling when he had made me moan like that last night.

'It's been a long day,' he said, taking an equally huge bite and chewing quickly. 'I'm tired. Might need an early night.' Ben didn't spot the subtext and I could only hope that my dad didn't either.

Behind his back, Erin grinned. If we had been friends I would have smiled back, but I still wasn't ready to make peace so I pretended not to notice. Instead I took another bite of my own dinner. A dollop of sauce dribbled out of the bottom and landed on my right boob. Eli picked up a napkin and leaned across the table. Behind him, my dad coughed and at the last second, instead of wiping it himself, he handed the cloth to me to clean up.

'Was it a shock to the system to go back to work after a week of sunshine?' I asked.

Ben brought his own plate and he and Erin came and joined us at the table. 'It was pretty quiet. The boss is still away so I spent some time building this new system.' He began to describe it. I understood roughly every other word. Erin was nodding along though so I tried my best to show that I cared even if I didn't take in the details.

We finished eating and I began to stack the plates. Dad fetched a bottle of the red wine that he had brought back from holiday and began to pour. 'Let's make the most of knowing that you're going to have a quiet spell and have a chat. I wanted to talk to you about something.'

'Should I go?' Erin asked, gesturing towards the door.

'Yes,' I told her.

'No,' Ben said, at the same time. I shot him a look but he either ignored it or didn't understand why I was still angry with her.

'Stay,' Dad told her. 'This affects all of you. As you know, Cody and I have been spending a lot of time together. I just wanted to check that you were all okay with that?'

'Dad,' I assured him, 'we're fine. You've been on your own for a long time. We're happy that you're happy, and Cody is great.'

He took a deep swallow of drink. 'I'm glad. You know how much I loved your mum. She was my everything, and after we lost her I thought I'd spend the rest of my life on my own. And I was okay with that.'

I thought back to how he had been before Cody had come into our lives; shuffling around like an old man, finding no pleasure in his existence. I looked at him now, with his purple Hawaiian shirt. Even without the suntan he would have been glowing. I wanted to tell him that Mum would have been happy to know that he was smiling again, but my memories of her were so vague that it would have been an assumption, and not a fact, so I kept quiet.

'Cody has been asked to take a series of photographs for an exhibition for the Mayor. She's nervous, it's the biggest commission she's had since she launched Picture Perfect.' Cody's new photography business had been the reason that we had got to know her, as she had launched her gallery across the road. I'd been nervous before I met her that another shop on our road might put my own business at risk. Now I knew how much she added to our family, I was embarrassed that I'd ever felt that way. I hoped Cody never found out how hard we had tried to investigate her before she moved in. Luckily Lily and I had been fairly inept in our early ventures and we'd found out very little before we'd met her for ourselves and halted the reconnaissance.

Cody also lived in the rooms behind her shop, but where our house was tall and thin, hers was deeper, with the kitchen tucked away at the back. Her front rooms contained displays of colourful and evocative images set against stark white walls, whilst her living spaces were full of colourful artefacts from her travels. I loved her home nearly as much as I adored her.

'I was thinking of going over to hers for a bit. Just to make sure that she doesn't get too stressed. There's going to be a big launch party fairly soon, a lot of bigwigs from the arts body that are funding the project,' Dad continued.

I began to understand why she was nervous. Cody had once been an award-winning journalist, but the pressure of being in war zones and natural disasters had led to her having a breakdown. Whilst she had recovered and showing photographs from her adopted city was half a world away from the issues that had caused her so much pain, it was probably the most public undertaking she had signed up for since. I could understand why Dad would want to make sure that she was looked after now.

'Is there anything we can do to help?' I asked.

He took a postcard from his pocket and handed it across. 'I think Cody wouldn't mind a few friendly faces at the launch show. It's a tight timescale. She's filling in for someone who has dropped out at the last minute. She said she'd normally have months to prepare, this time she has weeks and I think as it's quite a big event, she's feeling the pressure.'

I looked at the card that he offered. Cody had been asked to contribute to a celebration of London's diversity. As a newcomer herself, I looked forward to seeing through her lens how she perceived my city. I could think of no better person to capture the positivity and celebration of the many cultures that called this great place home.

'We'll be there,' I assured my dad, handing Eli the postcard. 'And in the meantime, maybe we can feed her, just to make sure that we're seeing her regularly?'

Dad cleared his throat. 'About that, I thought it might be easier to keep an eye on her if I spent a bit more time with her.' Now *that* I could understand. I was reminded of the relief that I'd felt when Eli had come in with me after our trip. Dad took another big mouthful of wine. His glass was almost empty, even though the rest of us had only taken a few sips from our own. He refilled it and began to pace the kitchen. 'Thank you for being so understanding. So, you won't mind if I go and stay with her for a while? I'll only be across the road after all.' I got the sense that he wasn't asking us, as much as he was telling us what he had decided.

But did we mind? I looked at Ben. He seemed fairly calm. I was glad that he didn't look more stressed at the possibility of change, although Dad hadn't mentioned how long he might be staying with Cody for. I wondered if that was a deliberate plan. It wasn't as though he was going far, either. We could practically see Cody's front door from our windows, if we peered down. Still, Ben was usually thrown by any changes to his routine. I looked at him again. Erin had taken his hand and was stroking it gently.

'If you need me to publicise the event, just let me know,' Ben offered. We all hurried to assure him that it would be fine. He meant well, but his idea of helping might not tally with our expectations. Ben was liable to hack a national newspaper website to add the event details, not thinking that there might be issues with crowd capacity, or privacy laws.

Dad patted his hand. 'I appreciate the thought, and Cody will be thrilled. If that's all, I'm going to pack a bag.' He left the room, whistling as he went.

Eli finished his wine and refilled his glass. 'I hope I'm still as excited as he is about shacking up when I'm his age.'

I glared at him. 'This isn't just about staying over at her house for a laugh. He wants to look after the woman he loves.' Eli had come a long way over the last few months from the playboy days of his past, but sometimes it infuriated me to realise that he still struggled to understand that sometimes people did nice things for the people they loved just because they wanted to. Since Eli's mum had passed away he'd had no family. Ben had been his only friend, and no matter how many times I told him and tried to show him unconditional love, he occasionally reverted back to the days when he couldn't believe that anyone could care about him enough to want to put themselves out for him. Suddenly I needed very strongly to show him how much he was loved. I stood up and walked over to him, resting my arms around him and kissing his cheek. He looked confused, obviously wondering how I could go from being cross with him one minute to being affectionate the next. I hoped that by demonstrating my love over and over, he would finally begin to trust that I wasn't going anywhere. He reacted to my closeness and pulled me onto his lap. Wrapping his arms around me, he nuzzled the back of my neck.

Erin reached across and kissed Ben's cheek too. He didn't move. He was too busy staring at his phone. 'Trouble.'

Chapter Eight

I let Taylor and Lily in and led them back to where the others were still waiting in the kitchen. Ben had fetched his laptop and returned to his seat next to Erin, but Eli hadn't moved. I could tell with one glance that the tension he had finally let go of on holiday had all come back and I itched to massage his shoulders, though I knew he would see it as a sign of weakness in front of Taylor. I sat on his lap and wrapped his arms around me instead so that I could be close to him.

'I've come straight from the office,' Taylor began.

Eli shot a glance at Lily. 'Don't worry,' she said. 'I wasn't there. I was coming to see if Daisy wanted to see a delivery that came into my store today.' Lily worked at what she called an 'adult entertainment and education experience', and what everyone else called a sex shop.

'That's very kind, but I don't think my customers have the same requirements as yours.' I'd once ordered a small sample of underwear from one of Lily's suppliers just in case my customers wanted something a little more adventurous without daring to go to her shop, but they hadn't sold well. I'd shifted a few sets every time a new *Fifty Shades* movie was released, but otherwise most of my customers leaned more towards the silk and luxury side of the market. Finally, when I'd almost given up on selling them, a customer had come and bought the remaining items for his wife. I'd been surprised, but he was a new customer and he had seemed determined that it was what he was after. He'd come in once more after that to buy his wife some earrings for Christmas, at which point he had mentioned that the underwear had had more holes and gaps than he had been expecting but that his wife, who if she was similar to her husband was probably also in her early eighties, had sewn up the crotch and the peepholes and now wore the sets very happily.

'Feel free to bring Daisy a personal supply. I'll settle up with you later,' Eli said. He grinned but it didn't reach his eyes and he released his hold of my waist, so I sensed that he was trying to ease the tension before Lily and I left them to talk work.

'Don't rush off,' Taylor said. I stayed where I was, but Eli didn't move to hold me again. 'If you try to listen in through the windows here you'd need a ladder, and I don't want any accidents on my conscience.'

We wouldn't have listened at the windows. We would have gone in to the living room and pressed our ears against the walls, though the old house had been solidly built and more than likely we would have barely heard a word.

Taylor continued his explanation. 'You remember me mentioning our French counterpart? The one that owes Ben a reward? He's gone missing.'

'Are you sure he hasn't just taken a holiday?' I asked, wondering whether anyone in their office ever knew where each other was. For a group of spies they seemed very *laissez faire* about disappearing without letting anyone know why. Maybe they actually enjoyed pretending to be extra-mysterious. I was beginning to find the whole thing rather frustrating.

'His department isn't like ours,' Taylor said. 'They're less secretive about what they do, and so they're a lot more accountable to their superiors. If they've missed him then he's really gone. His passport was still in his apartment in Paris, but we've had a possible sighting in London.'

'So, Ben can probably locate him if you give him a laptop and five minutes. What are they worried about?' It was snarky of me, but I still wasn't convinced that their Boss taking a few days off was really a good enough reason for Erin to have interrupted our holiday given how quickly Ben had found her, and I couldn't understand why they'd all be at panic stations again so soon for this. I really couldn't bear the idea of Eli losing his hard-found relaxation so quickly.

Eli shook his head. 'Ben's good, but so is this guy, and if he doesn't want to be found then ...'

'Fake papers? A secret mission?' Lily suggested. She was so excited at being included in the conversation that she was almost jumping up and down as she spoke.

'Contrary to what *James Bond* films would have you believing, those are rarer than you would expect.' Lily and I could be forgiven though for not understanding the impact of what Taylor said. Our first experiences of their hidden world had very much involved counterfeit passports and travelling.

'Do we know what kind of trouble he might be in?' Erin asked, obviously trying to get us back on track and distract us from thinking about the chase she had led us on previously.

'I was hoping Ben could check his online banking and see if he has made any withdrawals. He might uncover something that would give us a good starting point.'

Ben tapped away on his keyboard, looking intently at his screen. Erin gazed at him with adoration on her face. I knew I ought to start to try to like her, or at least to distrust her less for his sake, but I wasn't ready yet.

Ben paused for a moment, scratched his head, typed some more. Finally, he closed the lid and looked up. 'No recent withdrawals that would explain how he got here, but I did find something strange. He suddenly paid off the balance of his mortgage a few months ago and he's just paid a deposit for a new sports car.' Once again, I was reminded of how useful the internet was and how easily it gave up our secrets to the people who knew its tricks.

'I think we need to speak to the Boss. If he's here for a reason she needs to know about it,' Taylor said.

Eli agreed and I tried to hide how shocked I was. Lily held for no such subtleties, however. 'It must be bad if you two have stopped arguing,' she muttered, fetching a glass and helping herself to some of the wine.

'What do we do next?' Erin asked.

Taylor looked at her sheepishly. 'It's funny you should ask.' He went on to explain that no-one in the office had known where she was to give her the privacy she had obviously wanted, only that she had been located, but with the prospect of an agent going rogue in their territory he had had to disclose to her colleagues that Ben had traced her to the health retreat. I hoped that Ben wouldn't get into trouble for his illicit research, but consoled myself that not only did everyone in their office know Ben, but they employed him because of his unique skills, and so it shouldn't have come as any surprise.

'We've tried ringing the clinic, though they prefer to be known as a retreat or a spa, but they won't even confirm that she's staying. One of our agents drove over and even with his official documentation they wouldn't let him through the door.'

'Do you want me to hack the system and see if I can send her a message?' Ben asked.

'Given the urgency and secrecy that she left under, she probably won't have access to any of her electronic devices,' Lily pointed out. 'She might be really ill, maybe we need to give her this space?'

Taylor nodded. 'We've tried every messaging service she had on her phone, but she hasn't replied to a single one.'

'Want me to break in and see if I can talk to her?' Eli offered. 'If she does need longer off then we'll deal with it, but we can't decide that without talking to her ourselves.'

'She'd be very angry if you were to get caught,' I pointed out. 'Think of the publicity – secret agent caught breaking in to luxury retreat.' Eli began to argue that he was a trained specialist and had made it safely in and out of war-torn countries, a spa was unlikely to be as heavily protected, but Lily stopped him.

'I doubt those hell holes had CCTV linked to a private security firm. I knew I'd heard the name before, one of my best customers is an A-lister, very famous. She used to come in to buy supplies when she was first married, then she came back again and bought more when her marriage went through a tricky phase and she needed cheering up. She had great taste. I sold her this top of the range silicone ...' Lily stopped talking when Taylor gently tapped her knee to hint that she ought to move on. I was impressed that Lily had not told us this before. She wasn't known for being discreet. 'Anyway, when the marriage eventually ended, she went to stay there for a month until the press died down. She told me when she came back to see me, she started dating her newest co-star, I sold her the most enormous—'

'—La la la.' Ben put his hands over his ears as he sang.

'Anyway, the important thing is, the spa is for women only,' Lily explained.

'So, I guess one of us is wearing a wig and a dress and seeing if they'll let us in?' Taylor joked to Eli. Given that Eli was six-foot and Taylor was not only several inches taller but several foot broader, I hoped that he was joking.

'Don't you have any women at work?' I asked, gesturing at Erin. She flushed quickly and snuggled against Ben. Eli and Taylor turned to look at her.

'You'd be in and out really quickly. It would be like a holiday,' Eli suggested.

'You could get your hair done whilst you're there,' Taylor added. I winced at his bluntness, and Lily whacked his arm.

Erin touched her shoulder length bob nervously. 'It's fine,' I assured her. It was frizzy and needed a trim, but it wasn't polite to point it out. Besides, if she wanted to change anything, it would have made more sense to start with the pastel twin set she was wearing that would have been more suited to a woman several decades older.

'I couldn't,' she moaned. 'I'm not brave like you.'

'You'd only be going in long enough to find her and pass on a message,' Taylor said.

Erin got up and began to walk around, wringing her hands and grimacing. 'No. Definitely not. I can't.'

'The worst thing anyone will be armed with is a nail file or some waxing strips.'

Now I grimaced too. I'd still not forgiven Lily for trying to convince me that bikini waxes weren't painful. Ben opened his laptop and began to type. He turned the screen so that we could all see. There was a picture of a swimming pool. It looked as though it had been carved out of an underground cave and the photo showed it being lit up by candlelight. It was gorgeous. I sighed with longing.

'You can get spa treatments, seaweed wraps, facials,' Taylor read.

'Sign me up, I'll go,' Lily suggested.

'You don't know what she looks like.' That was just an excuse. They could have shown Lily a photo but none of them were brave enough to admit they were nervous of what Lily attempting to be undercover might look like. Except that it would not be subtle. 'She might be using a fake name,' Ben said without glancing up from the screen where he was now, looking at their prices and packages. He typed some more and the pictures disappeared, replaced by a list of what to me looked like random numbers, letters and symbols. I had no idea what I was looking at, but Ben pointed at something and looked triumphant. 'I could rig their fire alarms to go off. When they evacuate, we could sneak over and have a word.'

'If she's stressed then having one of you turn up like that might tip her over,' I joked. It probably wouldn't. I'd met her once when she'd unexpectedly turned up for a Christmas drink with her team when I'd gone to meet Ben. She was obviously made of sterner stuff, but just the fact that she had gone without telling anyone demonstrated that she needed a break and wasn't necessarily making decisions as well as she usually would.

'Then it's decided. Erin can go, we'll book her a weekend visit.' Erin wailed as Ben spoke. 'And Daisy can go with her, just in case.'

'And I can go too? I'd kill for one of their specialist massages. Do you know, my friend told me that they have one guy who uses his ...' I stuck my fingers in my ears as Lily spoke.

Chapter Nine

Swimsuit, yoga shorts, vest tops. I ran my finger down my checklist as I packed. Eli laid on my bed and watched.

'Are you sure you're okay about doing this?' he asked.

I folded a cardigan and placed it on top of my pyjamas. 'Did you see the rooms that Ben booked? I have a king-sized bed, I'm getting my nails done, it says they have a top chef on site who specialises in plant based cuisine. How could I possibly be anything other than happy right now?'

'Because you're going with Erin.' He knew me too well. 'Try not to sign her up for anything painful.'

I shot him a look, but he was right. Booking her in for a bikini wax wasn't especially mature. And it wasn't like Ben would care either way. He was besotted. 'I'll be polite, don't worry. I won't even sign her up for all the counselling sessions that they offer. We'll find your boss, update her, see if she has any ideas, and get out.'

'I wonder whether to try and sneak a mobile in so that you can let me know once you've spoken to her.'

'Lily says they search your bags. They get a lot of people who value their privacy, but we'll talk to her and then we'll be able to leave again. I'll be home before you know it.' I zipped the lid of my case closed and lifted it off the bed. 'I'll miss you.'

He opened his arms and I climbed into them. He kissed me, and I closed my eyes as I laid against his chest. 'I'd rather be with you,' I told him. 'It won't be the same being massaged by someone who lets me keep my pants on.' He laughed. 'Do you think we should be worried?' I continued.

'I'm not sure' he said. He rubbed his eyes and I looked at him closely. His dark skin had paled just a fraction but the bags under his eyes weren't as bad as they had been before we went away. I was glad. 'I'm sure she'll feel better after a break. I know I do. But it's not a good sign that she's gone off so quietly. It's a high-pressure job though. The risks of burnout are always present. As for our colleague from France, that's pretty troubling. If his bank account has suspicious transactions, that should have been flagged up. We don't expect people to double cross us, this isn't the cold war, but we deal with some pretty nasty types. We have to take some precautions, so perhaps he's on an undercover mission.' He shrugged.

'Is that likely?'

'Not really. Someone would know.'

'What do you think has happened?'

'Something somewhere has gone to shit.'

With that ringing in my ears I was as quiet as we climbed into Eli's car. He had managed to procure some false plates from work, but we decided that his car was as smart as a celebrity or titled lady might be expected to use so we hadn't sourced an alternative vehicle. He was wearing the grey suit again, aiming to look to any casual observers as if he were a chauffeur.

Ben was also dressed in a grey suit, though his was wrinkled and creased. He had paired his with a Sonic the Hedgehog T-shirt. 'Very smart,' I told him.

He looked confused. 'It's clean and it doesn't have any holes in. Eli told me to dress smart.'

I kissed his cheek and climbed into the back seat. 'Buckle up,' Eli called. 'We've got a short drive now to collect Erin but then it's going to take a couple of hours to get to the spa.' I sat back into the plush leather seats. Eli pressed a few buttons and the sounds of Ed Sheeran drifted out of the speakers. I was relaxing already. In the front Ben and Eli were discussing some of the projects that Ben wanted to work on. Eli cautioned him to wait until their Boss was back. I was glad that Eli was there to contain Ben's enthusiasm.

Goodness only knows what he would have set up if he was left to his own devices. We'd seen him come up with too many audacious plans in the past.

Ben, Eli and I had taken a trip to the United States once when we were teenagers. During our stay there were three news stories that had surprised me. The first had been the bombing of a women's health centre. That had been on the day that we first arrived. The follow-up piece the next day revealed that the bank account of the alleged group behind the attack had been emptied, leading to infighting and the attacker's identity and location being revealed to the police. On our final day, there was a small story at the end of the news stating that the health centre was due to be rebuilt and expanded due to an anonymous donation which had been received that week. There was no way of proving that Ben was behind the financial transactions, apart from the fact that he had been even more glued to his laptop than normal, but I had always suspected that he was. His sense of due process might be different to mine, but his ethical stance was unwavering and I loved him for it.

My lovely relaxed state faded when we picked Erin up. Luckily everyone seemed to accept my suggestion that she and Ben sit next to each other in the back as a kind gesture, and not just because I didn't want to spend any more time with her than I had to. She and Ben immediately snuggled up as close as their seatbelts would allow and began to whisper words of endearment to each other. I tried to do the same to Eli, but he just looked at me. I sighed. It was hard enough to get him to talk about his feelings in private. It was impossible to get him to say anything soppy in the car in front of people, even his best friend.

We drove north on the motorway for a long stretch, before Eli indicated and took an exit that twisted and turned, taking us deeper into the lush green countryside. June had brought with it plenty of rain, and though today was bright and clear, the lush plant life that bordered the road had clearly enjoyed it.

Eli navigated us down lanes that were barely wide enough for our car, and I almost screamed when a tractor trundled towards us, Eli managing to brake just in time to avoid hitting it, when I realised that the roads were in fact two-way. We drove a little slower after that, and the prospect of a couple of days of pampering seemed like it might be nearly enough to bring my pulse rate back down to normal.

I was just about to ask if we were nearly there when Eli pulled over into an unmarked dirt track and stopped. The only building in sight was a tumble-down wooden shed across the field. 'Doesn't look very luxurious,' I said.

'You need to get out,' Eli said. I stared at him. He stared back. 'Please?'

I unbuckled my seatbelt and climbed out, slamming the door behind me. Truthfully, I slammed it a little harder than I meant to. The car was Eli's pride and joy, and though I was pissed off with his bluntness, I didn't really want to do any permanent damage. To his car or to us. It had taken too long to get together with him to throw it away over his communication skills or lack of them. I stood waiting with my back pressed against the car, trying to work out what I was supposed to do or where I was supposed to go. I'd dressed carefully in a simple navy blue knee-length dress and matching sandals so that I would fit in with the posh crowd at the spa, but now the breeze was blowing up my skirt, and it wasn't the warm winds that we had enjoyed on holiday, I shivered.

Eli climbed out the car and closed his door, using a lot more care than I had. He walked round to me and held his arms out. I walked into them and he enveloped me in a hug. I rested my forehead against his broad chest, inhaling his aftershave as I leant in close. 'I'm sorry,' he began. 'I just meant that you and Ben need to swap places. It wouldn't do for the help to be riding in the back. I was just more blunt than I meant to be. We're a little tense at work about the implications if Jean-Luc really has gone rogue.'

'Is he seriously called Jean-Luc?'

'About as much as I'm called James Bond. You think I'm going to mention his real name? Everyone in the office is on edge, he's a really big deal in the French team. I've worked with calmer people who were being held at gunpoint.' I swallowed, shocked at the thought of Eli being in danger. He waved away my concerns with his hand. 'It doesn't happen often, don't worry. But for a long time my work was my life. After I lost my mum I was ...'

'Lost?' I suggested.

He nodded. 'I had Ben.' We both stopped to think about what comfort that would have been. Ben and Eli understood and loved each other like brothers, but Ben's idea of trying to cheer him up would have been to offer him a new computer game to play. 'Your dad tried his best too.' We both knew that this wouldn't have added much either. Dad was so consumed by his own grief that he would have had very little energy to help anyone through their issues.

'I wish we hadn't wasted so long being angry with each other.'

He kissed my head. 'I don't think I'd have been good for you back then. I was so angry. You were so sweet. Like your shop, you believe in romance and happy-ever-afters. I hate to think what spending time with me would have done to you.'

'You think you could have corrupted me any more than hearing some of the stories Lily tells me?' He laughed. 'But I guess I understand why you had to take your comfort where you could find it back then. I'm not entirely comfortable with how often you found it, but I get it.'

He kissed me again. 'I do love you, Daisy.'

Chapter Ten

This was the life. My flat was cosy, and it was nice to have my own space, but this was heaven. A bath. And not just any tub, this one had claw feet, and was currently filled almost to the brim with steaming water and rose-scented bubbles. Opening the brochure of possible treatments, I folded corners as I read about manicures and hot stone massages. I was just debating whether or not I'd enjoy a mud wrap when there was a knock at my door.

I didn't have a bath in my flat. I had to go upstairs to use Dad and Ben's bathroom when I wanted a soak usually, and so this was a real luxury and I didn't want to get out to see who it was. Instead I called out 'Hello?'

'It's me.' Erin. I could feel the relaxation fade. Sighing and knowing that I wasn't going to be able to enjoy myself anyway if I stayed in, I pulled the plug and tugged on the fluffy cotton dressing-gown that had been warming on the radiator. Erin slipped in as I opened the door. 'Have you seen the bathrooms? They're amazing.'

'I was just enjoying the bath.'

She came and sat on my bed, either ignoring or not realising that she had disturbed my relaxation. 'I've circled all the programmes that are most likely to have either a group of women or that might entice the Boss.'

'That's a good idea,' I admitted. 'I was just about to do the same.' She accepted my explanation without debate. I probably would have, to be fair, but not until I had soaked long enough for my fingers to be wrinkled like prunes.

'There's a group yoga class in an hour. I was thinking of going for a swim in the cave pool first. Do you know they have a candle-lit jacuzzi? I wish I could have brought Ben.' She giggled, and though it was odd to think of her and my brother together, she seemed to genuinely miss him.

'That sounds like a good plan. Why don't I grab my stuff and I'll come with you?'

There was no sign of her boss in the pool, but we didn't let that stop us from swimming a few languid laps. Erin wore an old-fashioned black all-in-one with long legs. In contrast my emerald-green bikini looked skimpy. It hadn't seemed anywhere near as small on holiday when I'd worn it next to Lily's hot pink outfit that had basically covered as much as three strips of dental floss. Erin seemed not to notice though, and she chatted away as we followed our swim with a laze in the bubbling jacuzzi.

'Do you think Ben would enjoy that?' she asked, and I realised that I had hardly heard a word that she'd said before. I asked her to repeat herself. 'A trip. To Ireland. But a planned one this time. I'd love for Ben to meet my parents. But this time I wanted to ask him first. And you. I think Eli might disappear me if I messed up and took him away without checking again.' She gulped and I wondered if she was really scared of Eli. I waited but she didn't speak again.

She looked so nervous as she waited for my answer that despite my reservations, I ended up nodding. 'I think Ben would love that.'

She squealed and launched herself across the water to give me a hug. 'I'm so excited.' I released her and glanced at the wall but there was no clock to be seen. I guess that was supposed to be relaxing, not worrying about the time, but we were also on a mission and if that needed us to take part in a calming yoga session, well, who was I to complain?

Ten minutes into the class I was very ready to yell at anyone who would listen. This wasn't like any group I'd ever been to before, and I'd been to a few. Lily and I loved going to yoga together when our shop opening hours allowed. These women were as bendy as a team of circus acrobats. 'Stand on your left leg, raise your right until your toes point to the ceiling, and hold while you breathe in for three, and out for three. And repeat.'

I wobbled. Next to me, Erin wasn't finding it any easier to copy. Her right leg wasn't lifted above her knee, and her left looked like it was shaking. 'I think I'm going to ... Aaargh.' She buckled, crashing into me and knocking us both to the floor.

I began to laugh. No-one else smiled. I looked at them; the lean, tanned women wearing outfits so tight you could tell that none of them ate regularly. I looked at my leggings that were baggy in the knee from being worn so often and Erin's jogging bottoms that looked suspiciously like a pair Ben often wore. Grinning, I took her hand and dragged her from the room. 'Sorry,' I yelled as we left. 'I think we'll go and find a beginners' class. We're not ready yet to be able to disappear up our own backsides.' Erin laughed and ran with me. We didn't stop giggling until we'd reached the café.

The spa claimed to be all-inclusive, and there was a buffet of healthy snacks on ice on a display table against the back wall. Perhaps many of the other guests shared our yoga class' attitude to food as no-one else was in the room. I loaded a plate with apple and melon slices and carried it to a table.

'I'd kill for a croissant and a coffee,' Erin said, staring at her own plate of salad.

'Lily sneaked a bag of chocolate truffles into my suitcase. She hid them inside a sanitary towel packet so the security guy didn't check it when he searched our bags. Let's finish this rabbit food and we can go and share them,' I said. She smiled again, and the ice between us began to thaw.

Back in my room I handed Erin the chocolates and picked up the brochure again. 'Safe to say that your boss probably isn't joining in the yoga.'

Erin unwrapped a chocolate and blushed a little. 'I think I farted when she asked us to do that thing with our backs.'

I laughed and helped myself to a truffle. 'I did too. The

lady behind me gave me such a dirty look. Thank goodness she was too posh to actually speak to me.'

'Where shall I try next?' Erin asked.

I looked through the brochure again. 'Pilates? Jazzercise?'

'I can't see the Boss at any of those,' Erin said. 'Not if she's here to unwind and de-stress.'

'There are individual therapy sessions. Maybe if you were to book one of those you could check out the rooms, see if there's any sign of her?'

'Why do I have to go? I've had my share of therapy. Besides, didn't they send you too so that I didn't have to go undercover? I can't. What happens if they ask why I'm there and I fold and tell them it's because I want to sneak a look in their files and find out if my boss is cracking up?'

'Or you could not mention that and try to look normal?'

She wasn't impressed by my answer and I was glad that I'd bitten back my first response of reminding her of her past as a kidnapper. Sighing in resignation, I went to the front desk and tried to look suitably sombre as I booked myself in for a session with the retreat's counsellor. It wasn't actually as hard as I thought it would be to look sad. I hadn't had any carbs since we had arrived and was on the verge of screaming anyway.

The girl behind the desk couldn't have been more than sixteen. She looked up at me with sympathy in her eyes and asked if I was willing to give a brief description of why I wanted to talk to a counsellor. I turned to look at Erin in a panic, hoping she could answer for me. I hadn't thought of what I was going to do when I got there. I was hoping that I'd walk to the therapy wing, spot the Boss and be able to duck out again. Still, with the loss of my mum and the length of time that Eli and I had bickered before we got together, I ought to be able to reassure the girl that I needed to talk to a therapist. She looked at me expectantly, her smart white blouse showing not a wrinkle, even where it was tucked into her black knee-length skirt. I'd never felt quite so well put together, and wondered how much of that was due to not having my mum around to teach me how to dress up. I was just about to explain that I was there to talk about my bereavement issues, when Erin leaned past me and whispered 'she's a sex addict.'

In her soft Irish burr it didn't sound quite as bad, and yet I still yelped and shot her a glare. The girl behind the desk didn't bat an eyelid. She typed a few buttons on her screen and then looked up and smiled. I couldn't meet her eyes. 'Our sex addiction specialist actually has a free slot today.' I tried not to laugh at her innocent innuendo. 'You're lucky, he's usually booked solid.' How many sex addicts did they have here?

'Unless you'd prefer to see a woman?' the girl continued. 'Some of our patients find talking to a man about this a little distracting.' She paused and looked both ways, making sure that the corridor was deserted before letting out a little giggle. 'Robert really is quite good-looking. Erm, Dr Porter, I mean.'

'I'm sure he'll do just fine,' I muttered, trying to not glare at her. If we didn't find the Boss in the next hour I was going to have to fake an hour's worth of sex addiction face to face with a hunk. I could only hope that I remembered every story Lily had told me.

Chapter Eleven

'You didn't think to go with me losing my mum? *Sex addiction*? What were you thinking?'

Erin wisely decided that shouting this out loud in the main atrium probably wasn't my wisest move and she shepherded me into her room. Burrowing into her suitcase, she brought out a giant box of tampons. 'Hurrah.'

'I've never been that happy to get my period.'

She opened the box and drew out a small bottle of whisky. 'I had the same idea that you did when Ben warned me that they were going to search our bags. I tried hiding an old mobile inside my bag too but they found it. On the bright side, they were so happy to confiscate the phone that they didn't look any further.' She fetched the glasses from the bathroom next to her toothbrush. You could tell this place was classy; they were proper cut-glass tumblers, not those plastic cups in wrappers that you get in the hotels I usually stayed in. Cracking open the bottle, she poured me a hefty dose and handed it over.

I took a sip. It was rich and peaty. I took another mouthful. Or maybe two. My glass was mysteriously empty. 'I may have misjudged you, Erin,' I told her. 'All we need is some chocolate. I'll be right back.' In my room, I quickly wrapped the packet in a hand towel so that no sign of my contraband was on show and took the box back into Erin's room. I handed her the chocolates and she gave me a fresh shot of whisky.

'How long before my session?' I asked, lying back on Erin's bed and closing my eyes.

'An hour.'

'We'd better get planning. What exactly am I going to say?'

But it was no use. The time flew by in a blur of alcohol and sugar. The salad leaves that we had been fed for lunch were in no way a decent cushion for the amount of straight spirits that I was downing.

Erin hiccupped. 'Time to go.'

'I want pizza,' I said, sitting up to find that the room had started to spin around me. 'How much did we drink?'

The corridors were still empty. There must have been a legs, bums and tums session on, not that any of the women I'd seen here had a tummy, let alone dared to have even an ounce more on their bottom than they had in their teen years. Erin was decidedly more steady on her feet than I was, and after I crashed into the wall for the third time she took my arm and guided me back to the therapeutic wing.

At the counter, I looked for the girl who had booked me in, but she was nowhere to be seen. I leaned over the counter to see if there was any paperwork on show, but the desk was disappointingly clear. Some people were too efficient for my purposes. Except, on the floor, almost hidden was an access card. I ducked around and picked it up. 'Tell me if anyone comes,' I hissed to Erin, before lifting the phone off the desk and beginning to dial. 'It's not working.'

'Try pressing nine for an outside line. That was the code in every office I ever temped in,' Erin suggested.

I did as she said, before typing in Eli's mobile number. It rang twice before he answered. Sounding a little suspicious, he said hello but didn't give his name. 'Do they teach you that at super spy school?' I asked him. 'How to answer your phone and not give away who you are?'

'Daisy? Are you okay?'

'I'm better than okay,' I told him. 'Shhh, I'm a little drunk.' He sighed down the phone. 'I thought you liked drunk Daisy? Drunk Daisy does fun stuff. Not this drunk Daisy though. I miss bread.'

He took a deep breath; it rattled down the handset. 'Is there any sign of the Boss?'

'Nope, no, nah.'

'Have you been looking or drinking?'

'I looked. I looked in yoga. No-one there except a bunch of women who were trying not to fart but from their faces you could tell they all needed to.'

'And in the rest of the spa?'

'Not in the pool, even in the candlelit area. I want to swim there with you. It's so romantic. There's lots of dirty things I want to do with you there.' I dropped my voice down to a whisper. 'Lily told me some stuff to try. I was too scared when she suggested it, but now I think it might be fun.'

'Is Erin there?'

I handed her the handset. I couldn't hear his voice anymore, only her responses. 'No, no sign. Only a couple of small shots. I have no idea how she's so drunk. I'm fine. Maybe it's the lack of food.' I took the handset back from her again.

'I have to go and talk to some cute guy about my sex addiction. I'll call you soon. Bye. Ooh, also we found a swipe card thingy. Okay, bye.'

I went to hang up, but Erin stopped me, grabbing the phone and pulling it to her ear before tugging it sharply away as Eli bellowed my name down the line. She listened for a moment, made some noises of agreement and hung up. She had just come around the desk and begun to try and lift me up from the floor when the girl came out of the staff bathroom and spotted us.

'Just having a quick rest while we wait for Doctor Gorgeous to talk to me about sex.'

She looked at us suspiciously as Erin continued to drag me off the floor. Her final tug was hard and sent me flying, landing on top of her just as the door to the therapy room opened.

'Daisy?'

Erin and I looked up. I tried to climb off her, but she was all nylon and bones and I slipped over, taking an accidental elbow to the forehead in the process. Rubbing my head, I managed to slide off and sit on the floor. Stood in front of us was one of the most gorgeous men I had ever seen. He was around six-foot, blond and clean-shaven. He wore a pale blue shirt and black trousers, no tie – probably to show that he wasn't too formal and that his clients could be relaxed with him. I licked my lips. I could fake a sex addiction if I was talking to him. Only talking, mind you. I was happily taken these days, but a girl can look. In fact, next to me Erin was looking too.

I dug a tissue from my pocket and handed it to her. 'Wipe your mouth. You're drooling.'

We both scrambled to our feet. I was about to follow the counsellor into his room when Erin took my arm. 'You look a lot better now Daisy. Are you sure you still need to talk to someone?'

'I think I do.'

'It's just that there's somewhere else we need to be. I think we've accidentally double booked ourselves for the massages too.' She turned to the staff. 'We're really sorry about that. If Daisy relapses and wants to talk about sex with you, erm, I mean, talk about her sex addicition with you, I'll be sure to bring her back.'

She tugged me around the corner. As soon as we were out of sight she began to run, not stopping until we were back in the spa area, near the massage rooms. We bent over to catch our breath.

'Maybe I should sign up for a few more exercise classes after all,' I said, doubled over and trying to breathe. I straightened up and the alcohol reached my brain again, sending me a big wave of dizziness.

'Have you got the access card?' Erin asked. I tried to

remember what she was talking about, but my brain was still addled by booze and hunger. 'The swipe card?' Finally her voice pierced the fog in my mind and I handed it across. She took it and shoved it underneath the fire exit door. I looked at her in surprise, but she didn't explain. 'Let's see if we can find you some proper food,' she said, taking my arm and guiding me back to the buffet. 'We've got a few minutes to spare.'

I wanted to ask what she meant, but she was too busy handing me a plate and loading it with food.

'It's all green,' I moaned. 'When they said plant-based I hoped they meant more than just leaves.'

'That's all they have. Maybe if you eat enough it'll sober you up.' I shrugged and began to try and consume the vast pile of salad. She had sprinkled some extra seeds on top and they added some much-needed crunch, but it still didn't make for a satisfying meal. Sighing, she took the plates and carried them over to the counter, before handing me a tall glass of water.

'Drink that, you'll thank me when the whisky wears off.'

She led me back over to the spa area. 'What are we doing?' I asked her.

'It should be about the right time.'

'For what?'

'Me,' said Eli, opening the door to a massage room and inviting me inside. He was wearing a tight white T-shirt and matching trousers. 'You booked for a full body rub?'

I launched myself at him.

Chapter Twelve

It wasn't until we had caught our breath and I had climbed off Eli, the massage table creaking under our weight, that I thought to ask him what he was doing there. 'I thought that you and Ben couldn't get in, that was why you needed me and Erin on the inside?'

'The swipe card you found, we picked it up from outside the fire exit and let ourselves in.'

'Ben's here too?' Eli nodded. 'And he'll be okay? He won't get caught and give everything away? He's not good under pressure.'

'Erin is next door with him. I'm sure she'll be careful.'

'I think I underestimated her.' I smiled, thinking about how I was finally getting to know her a little. 'But why are you here? We haven't found your Boss yet.'

'You mentioned being in desperate need.' I raised an eyebrow at him. 'Of carbs.' He opened a cupboard door and took out a box of pizza. I groaned. 'And there was me thinking that it was just my body that made you make noises like that. Please remind me to thank Lily for the lessons too. That thing you did with your leg, that was amazing.'

I ignored him, concentrating instead on my food. I was two slices in before I turned to look at him again. 'This can't be very attractive. Sorry.' I had sauce down my chin and cheese on my T-shirt.

'I don't know. If you looked at me the way you're looking at that pizza I don't think I'd mind. You sounded a little drunk on the phone. I was going to check that you really wanted to, but you already had my trousers off.'

I finished my third slice and took a fourth. 'Did you want some too?' Eli shook his head. 'I wanted to. Did I not make that clear? Let me eat some more carbs and I'll show you again. Wow, it feels good to have some proper food in my belly.' He watched me eat in silence for a few more minutes. 'There's no sign of your Boss yet though, I'm afraid. We've hung out in the pool, the buffet, we tried exercise classes. That's why we signed up for therapy; the counselling is in a separate wing and it was the only way we could think of to go and have a look there.'

'And the sex addiction? Not that I'm complaining.'

I grinned and looked around us. The room was sparsely decorated. The massage table was covered in clean white towels. The walls were painted a dark grey. A counter ran along one wall, holding candles and various pots and jars of creams. Underneath that was the row of cabinets that Eli had hidden my pizza in. Against the back wall was a door leading to a tiny shower cubicle. I saw it and looked at Eli.

We took the towels from the table to dry ourselves with afterwards. I found a clean set of scrubs in a cupboard and swapped my dirty T-shirt. It wouldn't do to get caught out by a stray food stain. He gave me one more big kiss and let me go. 'I'll be nearby, just ring again if you need me. We'll hang on to the card so we can get in again just in case.'

'I can't ring easily. They're so worried about keeping everything inside confidential. Ben was right, they searched our bags. They took Erin's phone.'

'But not her whisky, clearly.'

The beginnings of a hangover were reminding me of that. Eli pulled a mobile from his pocket and handed it to me. 'Now that you're in you should be okay, I don't think they'll search you again, if you could try not to be too obviously drunk! This one is untraceable. Call if you need us.'

I let myself out and began to make my way back to my bedroom. I'd just reached the bar area when Erin called me. She was sat holding a martini glass containing something pink and fruity. She offered me one, but I waved it away. 'No more alcohol for me, thanks.'

'There is none,' she said, not looking happy about it. 'It turns out that this place also specialises in alcohol addiction, and so the whole facility is dry.'

'Oops,' I said, making a mental note that I'd have to hide my hangover in the morning. I took a seat next to her and signalled to the waiter for my own drink. I took a sip. It had a sharp tang of citrus, enough to make my eyes water. I pushed it away.

'Did you come up with a plan?' she asked.

'Erm, did you?'

We both blushed and reached for our drinks at the same time. I grinned, until I realised that it meant that she had been intimate with my brother in the next room. That was unsettling enough, but I couldn't remember whether I'd been very quiet. Hopefully if anyone heard us, they'd have thought it was just people really enjoying their massages.

'I've got a phone,' I whispered. 'If we find her, I can call Eli.'

'But did you come up with a plan of how to do that?'

I had not. I had been distracted. Perhaps a quick session with the therapist was in order after all.

'Back to plan A,' she said, handing me a brochure and a pen. 'I'll go to jazzercise. That looks like a busy class. Should be a good chance to see if she turns up. Why don't you wait in the buffet? She's got to eat at some point.'

That felt like a less frustrating experience now that my belly was happily full of carbs. Erin was about to slip off her seat when I stopped her. 'Don't turn around, but I think your Boss just walked in.'

Erin flushed again and picked up her glass, trying to hide behind the slice of pineapple and colourful cocktail straws as she drank. I peeked behind her. A middle-aged lady wearing black Lycra shorts and a tight black T-shirt sat on the next barstool.

'I'll take the closest thing you have to a vodka martini,'

she told the bartender. Her grey hair was tied back in a messy pony-tail. Erin's eyes were bugging out of her head. I thought it was her Boss – the cut-glass accent sounded familiar – but I'd only ever seen her once, dressed in a power suit, her hair in a sleek bob, not a single strand out of place.

The bartender set a glass in front of her. The liquid inside was clear, and two olives were skewered on a cocktail stick. There, sadly, all resemblance to a cocktail ended. She lifted it to her lips and her eyes closed in anticipation, until she took a sip and clattered the glass back onto the table.

'On what planet does that resemble a martini?'

'It has olives,' the bartender said, his face turning paler than his white shirt.

'In what appears to be, if I'm not mistaken, water.' She looked down her nose at him and I presumed that she wasn't in the habit of being wrong.

He took the glass away and handed her a menu. 'This is a dry facility. I'm sorry. I can offer you a fresh squeezed orange juice, a Virgin Mary, a long island iced tea, also virgin.'

'Which would basically be a glass of overpriced cola and ice?'

The bartender's anxiety levels began to increase. I could see his hands shaking. How she managed to work with Ben without killing him, I had no idea. 'I can get my manager,' he squeaked. He let himself out from behind the bar and headed to the atrium.

I climbed down from my chair and turned to whisper to her. 'We have whisky if you want to come to our room.'

Chapter Thirteen

'I should have known that Eli and Ben would be behind this,' she said, but it didn't stop her from taking the glass that Erin handed her and sitting herself in the only armchair. Erin poured herself another glass of whisky, but I'd brought my fruit juice from the bar so I stuck with that.

'We didn't mean to interrupt your trip,' Erin began.

'Well, we did. But we didn't want to. It's just that Jean-Luc is in the UK. Apparently, he's been acting suspiciously and no-one knows what to do. I don't even know what his real name is. Eli wouldn't tell me.'

'I know the Captain he's talking about,' she assured us. 'I assume that I don't want to know how Ben tracked me down?'

We shook our heads. I handed her a chocolate and she chewed on it as she thought. 'James Bond on a bike, I only came for a few days' peace and quiet.'

Erin and I began to apologise again but she waved us away. 'I was bored anyway. It turns out that the thought of non-stop relaxation and herbal tea is a lot more enticing in theory. I am so bloody bored. I even made a waiter cry this morning when they wouldn't bring me a cup of coffee. What kind of place doesn't serve caffeine?' She took another hit of whisky.

I wanted to caution her that it was strong stuff when you only had access to salad to line your stomach, but the expression on her face stopped me from interfering. 'So, you two are in relationships with Eli and Ben?' We nodded. She picked the bottle of whisky up from where Erin had left it. 'You must be in need of some of this too.' She topped both glasses up and we sat in silence, drinking. I tried to make mine last as long as possible, but every time her own glass was empty she topped mine up as well.

Eventually I gave up trying to look sober, set my glass on the bedside table, tucked myself under Erin's duvet and fell asleep. I woke up the next morning with Erin's feet on the pillow next to me. It was a little odd, but it would have been more strange to wake up looking into her eyes. My head was pounding, and my stomach felt as though it was full of battery acid. I groaned. In the armchair, I heard a moan being returned right back to me. Sitting up, I rubbed my eyes and came face to face with my brother's boss.

Her hair was standing on end and her once pristine gym wear was now creased and dishevelled. She opened her eyes, looked at me and then ran into the bathroom, locking the door behind her. A moment later I heard retching, and then the tap running. I dug Eli's phone from my pocket and rang him. He picked up quickly and I wondered whether he'd slept at all.

'The good news is, we found the Boss. But we're going to need coffee. And pastries.'

I met Eli by the fire exit. Today he was dressed in black trousers and a blue shirt. It was a good outfit; he looked like one of the orderlies and could have snuck in and pretended to be anything we needed. With his handsome face and confident poise most people would have believed him.

'Did you need any more help with your sex addiction?' he asked, handing me a tray of drinks and a bag of food. I hid them both under a towel and kissed his cheek.

'Maybe later. If you packed some painkillers for my headache and if there is enough grease in here to settle my tummy. You didn't mention that your boss likes a drink. I'll take these back quickly before she emerges from the bathroom and I'll ring when we know what the plan is.' I made to walk away but he called me back and kissed me once more. It was the kind of kiss that sends tiny ripples of electricity right down to your toes.

'When we're finished here, we definitely need to talk about what else Lily has taught you.'

I flushed at the promise of future delights.

Back in the room, Erin was just waking up and I handed her a paper cup of coffee. The heat stung her fingers and she sat it down quickly, blowing on her finger-tips. I apologised but she waved it away.

'Anyone who brings me coffee is a friend of mine. But goodness me the Boss can put away the whisky. Where is she?'

I pointed at the bathroom where I could now hear the shower running. She emerged just as we opened the bag of food and began to unpack the pastries and muffins. Somehow, despite having no change of clothes or toiletries with her, she now looked fresh and put together again. I handed her a cup, and she accepted it gratefully. Blowing on the surface, she sipped it and breathed a sigh of relief.

'Perhaps your young men do have their uses after all.' I didn't tell her the uses I had in mind for Eli when we finally got out of here. Instead I handed her a poppy seed muffin and waited for her to tell me what to do. 'I need to ring someone,' she said. 'I've an old friend. Not a direct colleague of "Jean-Luc's".' I could sense, rather than see the quotation marks around the code name Eli had used for him. 'That would raise too much suspicion. My friend can investigate if anything unusual is happening around his office. Now, there are no public phones on site so I might need to break out for a little while.' She glanced at the coffee and raised an eyebrow. 'Of course, you had to communicate to arrange breakfast. I take it you have arrangements in place for making contact?' I handed her Eli's phone. She made a quick call, slipping into fluent French as she greeted her friend. She soon hung up, and I wondered whether everybody who met her agreed very quickly to do as she asked. Her poise certainly suggested that they did, and when she looked directly at me, I found myself sitting up straighter and waiting for my own orders.

'Is there any more coffee?' That wasn't what I was expecting. I shook my head.

'I can call and get more. In fact, now that you know what's going on, Erin and I can go. I'll ask Eli to drop more off when he picks us up. Would you like to come with us?'

She shook her head. 'I might keep the phone though, if you don't mind. I'm not surprised that Keith hasn't managed to control the office without me, he always was a bit of a damp squib. It wouldn't surprise me if he's so panicked that he's got the whole office hyped up and in a state.' It was chillingly close to the description that Erin and Eli had given of the atmosphere in her absence. 'Now I can keep in touch and tell him what he ought to be doing, then I can treat myself to a manicure to relax again afterwards. It's a win-win situation.'

I asked for the mobile back for a moment so that I could text Eli and update him of our plans. 'If we pack up, I can ask them to pick us up in a few minutes,' I said to Erin.

'I assume that Ben booked you in and is making sure that you don't face an excessive bill when you check out?' the Boss asked us.

I looked at Erin to see if she knew how we ought to respond to that question, but she didn't answer.

'Why not let them know that you're coming out soon but take the time for one more treatment before you go? Goodness knows that putting up with those two, you both deserve a little pampering.'

Chapter Fourteen

Eli kissed my cheek and opened the door. I was trying to hold on to the relaxation from my trip for as long as I could, but a little of it left as soon as he went to work. I knew that Eli had been happier about going back now that the Boss was behind the scenes directing them again. He was expecting to hear back from her contact soon to find out if anything looked suspicious. Or more suspicious than we already knew about at least.

I tried to distract myself from worrying by tidying my flat up. Eli hadn't caught Ben's tidiness any more than I had, and within the cramped confines of my room it showed. Picking up my skirt from the day before, along with a pair of Eli's socks that had somehow worked their way under my bed, I loaded a basket and carried it up to my dad's flat.

It was quiet up there, with Dad staying at Cody's and Ben at Erin's. The sound of the washing machine rumbling echoed off the walls in the absence of any noise to distract from it. I made myself a mug of Dad's posh coffee and carried it back down to my flat. My shop wasn't due to open for another hour, but I hadn't changed my window display for some time, and the summer sun had begun to bleach the colour from the origami flower display that Cody had made for me.

I moved the paper roses in their crystal vase and put them on a shelf where they were out of the direct sun. In their place I carefully arranged an empty champagne bottle that I'd saved from mine and Eli's three-month anniversary earlier in the year. When it has taken you ten years to finally get together, you celebrate every month.

Next to that, I carefully laid a CD of the song that had been playing when Eli and I had first got together, all those years before. We'd listened to it on Valentine's Day. I'd given him a box of his favourite cakes. His mum used to make an amazing ginger cake, and Dad and I had worked hard to recreate it. He'd liked them, but he'd enjoyed the underwear set that Lily had picked out for me even more.

In return he'd given me a card that he had clearly bought at the last minute when he realised that I'd be expecting one. He struggled with traditional notions of romance. It had made for interesting debates in the past about the purpose of my boutique. He also frowned on overcrowded and overpriced restaurants cashing in on the act, as he called it, but he'd tried to make up for this by bringing a takeaway, wine and condoms. It might have been a tad more romantic if he had also brought candles and flowers, but I had those anyway. And we made the most of it. He knew I was tired after the months of planning I'd put into making everyone else's day special, so he'd also bought me a new romantic comedy DVD and given me the best back rub I'd ever had. He took me out for a meal the following day to my favourite restaurant when it was much less busy. He'd been more comfortable, and we'd had a wonderful time.

I added a sprinkling of gems to my window display and some lace hearts, like those that had decorated the tables at the wedding we had been to shortly before we got together. It was a little more cliché than most of my displays, and yet at the same time more personal. I was tempted to add a photo of Eli but that felt just a little too public. Mind you, the most successful day my shop had ever had with new clients had been the time that Eli and Taylor had nearly come to blows outside in the street and a group of passing girls had come to watch them and had left with bags of gifts.

I checked my watch. Mr King was due in ten minutes. I put the kettle on and arranged some of Dad's homemade shortbread, baked yesterday and topped with cream and fresh berries from the fruit market. Dad had dropped them off the night before but hadn't come in for dinner. Cody had been out taking photographs for the show and he'd wanted her to come home to some treats and a hot meal. Most likely he'd also been checking up on us, but he did so very tactfully and it felt really lovely to have him be cheerful enough once again to think to do so.

Mr King had previously been the kind of client I dreaded, and at the same time needed. He wasn't afraid to spend significant amounts of money; he was just very, very selective about what he spent it on. He had been known to look through every item in my shop, until I had asked him whether he was even sure that he wanted to buy from me at all. At Christmas though inspiration had struck, and I had set him up with a family photo shoot to celebrate the birth of his youngest grandchild.

It seemed that his years of working at a top bank in London had allowed him to already purchase most of the material items that people usually came to me to buy. This time I was prepared for him. I'd put together a new plan. I'd once organised a celebration of a couple's wedding, complete with a restoration of a long-lost piece of music. Now I had an entire folder complete with romantic meal ideas, vow renewals and holidays. I was going to offer complete packages, from flowers for the lady to be delivered in advance of the date, perhaps an outfit or piece of jewellery. Following that, I had several local restaurants who had agreed to make any favourite dishes that might be required that weren't on their regular menu. I had even contacted a luxury car dealer who was prepared to escort my clients to their special occasions.

I felt so prepared for the visit, that when he discarded every one of my carefully sourced and selected gift ideas from my shelves, it didn't faze me at all. When he strode around my shop, walking stick tucked under his arm like a swagger stick, I barely broke a sweat. Instead, I poured him a second cup of black coffee into the bone china mug and whipped out my new folder.

He took a sip, set the cup on the glass counter and gave his trousers a quick flick so that they didn't crease when he sat down.

'We eat out regularly, so a meal isn't going to cut it,' he sniffed, turning a page in the binder.

A slight sweat broke out on my forehead. It was tempting to send him down to the big central London department stores and leave him to fend for himself, but I reminded myself that he was here because he wanted my help, so I took a sip of my own drink, wished that it was alcoholic, and set my shoulders square ready to do battle with his reluctance.

'Mr King,' I began, 'did you have any ideas that you wanted me to help with?' If only it could be so easy.

He looked up, frowning as he spoke. 'If I knew that I wouldn't be here.' He turned another page and glared at what he read. I went and fetched some chocolate biscuits. It was clearly going to be one of those visits after all.

By the time he had read my entire file of research and found no ideas, I was deep in a daydream where I'd taken my cup and swapped the coffee for vodka. He gave a gentle cough, and I sat upright again, trying to will my brain come up with a genius idea that would make him happy and also make him leave.

'We've just got back from a week in China, Mrs King had always wanted to see the Great Wall,' he said, by way of explaining that a weekend in Paris or Barcelona wasn't what he was after. 'And we're at that new Michelin star place tonight for a product launch that my firm has been involved with.' So a meal round the corner at the tiny bistro with their reclaimed wood tables and jam jar glasses was definitely not going to cut it, even if the chef was prepared to make their favourite food. Mr King would probably prefer some fiddly gastronomic delight. Being able to request a taste of their childhood was clearly not elegant enough for a man of his position.

I stood up from my stool and began to pace the floor. Given that all of my carefully prepared ideas had come to nothing, I simply rambled as I walked, hoping that something might catch his attention.

'So, what do we know that Mrs King likes? She has a sense of humour. More naughty toys?' He didn't speak. I took this as a negative. 'But for your anniversary a funny gift alone is obviously not suitable. We know that she likes jewellery.' Still no reply. 'But she has an impressive collection already and is unlikely to be suitably impressed by a new item on its own. She enjoyed the photo shoot.'

'She did,' Mr King said, and I hoped that this meant that I was on to something. 'That was an inspired idea of yours.'

Right now, I would kill for another one. 'Would she like another photo shoot, this time with just the two of you perhaps?'

He shook his head. 'She enjoyed the last shoot, but mostly because it was celebrating the birth of Mathilda. Mrs King has been so looking forward to becoming a grandmother.' The hint of a smile that accompanied the memory soon passed though. 'It has been the cause of some tension recently. My wife had been hoping to have a Christening party. She had offered our son to use our house if he wanted to hold it at the Church where he was christened, but he and his wife are not religious. I can understand that, it's a different world now to the one I grew up in, though of course I would choose for them to be more involved.'

I kept my mouth shut. It's not like I was religious myself. Dad had lost any lingering elements of his religious upbringing when we had lost my mum, and so I hadn't been brought up with any particular beliefs. 'How about a non-religious celebration?' I suggested.

I didn't think he would agree. Not that I was an expert, but there were spiritual elements of a Christening that would be missing without the Church, but he seemed interested so I continued. 'You could still host it, have many of the same elements, the cake and champagne, but it allows your children to mark the event in a personal way. And Mrs King might enjoy hosting.'

He clapped his hands together and stood up. 'And you'll help? With the decorations and so forth?'

'I will,' I assured him, 'if this is something that both your wife and your son's family would like? It isn't exactly what either of them had in mind, and I don't want to be the cause of more family distress.'

'Nonsense,' he said, standing up and reaching for his jacket, even though the weather was pleasantly warm. 'We'll set a date and be in touch.'

I closed the shop after he left. It was impossible to settle to do anything. I couldn't help but worry that I'd set him up to both upset his wife, who still wouldn't be getting the religious ceremony that she wanted, and his son who might feel that this party was being forced on him. I pottered around my flat trying to organise it a bit more but I'd not long cleaned it, so it didn't take me as long as I had hoped.

After hanging up my laundry, I made another cup of tea and tried to distract myself by looking for more stock online, but when I found myself looking up 'It's a girl' banners and balloons, which I knew Mr King would find far too tacky and lacking in class, I shut down my laptop and treated myself to a nap.

Eli woke me up, kicking his shoes off, dropping his tie on the floor next to the bed and climbing in next to me. 'Tough day at the office?' he asked.

'You have no idea,' I groaned. He cocked one eyebrow. 'Okay, you probably have a very good idea. But whilst I didn't have to deal with terrorists or explosions, I fear I might have inadvertently caused World War Three in Surrey.' I explained about my idea for Mr King's wife.

'It sounds like a wonderful compromise,' he said.

'It is, but religion isn't something people tend to compromise on,' I pointed out. 'How would your mum have felt if we had children and didn't get them christened?' He shuddered. Perhaps it was thinking about how his mum would have reacted, or perhaps it was the thought of the level of commitment it would take to have children. I moved the conversation on swiftly.

'See,' I told him. 'Now tell me about your day, or whichever bits of it you're allowed to share. Distract me from my mistakes by telling me that there's nothing strange going on in Paris.'

'Let's see. What can I safely tell you about my day? I had a sandwich for lunch. Does that help?'

Chapter Fifteen

I didn't sleep well. It might have been the long afternoon nap, or it might have been worrying about what I'd suggested to Mr King. After I woke Eli up for the third time with my tossing and turning, he did his best to help tire me out, and though he slept well afterwards, I still did not. Instead I let myself in to Dad's flat and curled up on his sofa with a blanket and watched some terrible old films until it was time to get up for the day, at which point I promptly fell asleep again.

The advantage of running my own business was that there was no-one to tell me off for opening up three hours late. The disadvantage was that there was no-one to step in and take over when Mr King turned up, without an appointment, and sat himself down at my counter. I put the kettle on, stalling for time and hoping that he wasn't here to shout at me.

Thankfully he wasn't. Surprisingly his family were very happy at my suggestion, and he had come to arrange a date and pay a deposit for my help. By the time he left I felt utterly drained, but I decided to try and manage without a nap in the hopes that I'd be able to sleep better that night.

This time I was awake when Eli got home from work. I immediately wished that we'd had time for a nap. He looked exhausted. I handed him a bowl of spaghetti bolognese. He covered it in cheese and dug in. I waited until he had eaten half of it before I asked whether he could tell me what had happened.

He watched me eat some of my dinner and looked confused. 'How can you be eating this?' he asked. It was my turn to look confused.

'It's my dinner.'

'It's spag bol. You're vegetarian.'

'It's made with Quorn mince instead of meat.'

He looked at his nervously after that, though he had eaten so far without any complaints. Finally he sighed, and then continued digging in. Afterwards he washed up whilst I poured him some wine. He didn't open up until after his glass was empty.

'The Boss is back.'

'She had enough of relaxing and wanted a proper meal and a decent Merlot?'

'Her friend found something. Taylor and I are off to France.'

I'd never known where he was going before, and rarely heard more even once he was safely back. Suddenly the room felt cold. I rubbed my arms to try and warm them. Eli crossed to me and held me against him. 'Will it be safe?' I asked, not wanting to look at him in case he gave me any indication that it wasn't.

'It should be,' he assured me. 'It seems to be some financial discrepancies at the moment. Ben found them today, they were pretty well hidden, but the Boss wants us to go and meet her friend and check a few things out. I should be back by Friday. I'd better get moving. She goes nuts if we're late.'

'You're going now?'

'No rest for the wicked.' Or the tired and harassed it seemed.

He walked into the bedroom, packed a small bag and stopped to give me a kiss, before letting himself out the front door. I called Lily.

'Are you on your lonesome too?' I asked when she answered.

'Get out!' Lily yelled. 'Those changing rooms are for one person at a time.' Her voice dropped back down to a regular volume and I rubbed my ear better. 'Honestly, were they both trying to fit into that cat suit at the same time? They think they're the first people to think of sneaking in. If I have to clean up after one more ...'

I interrupted. I didn't want to know what she'd had to clean up before. 'Eli grabbed a bag and he and Taylor are off for a few days.'

'I got a text,' she said. 'I'm on my own now if you want to come over? I'm here 'til we close at midnight but you're very welcome to join me. I've got a few boxes from a new factory to price up. One of the boxes keeps vibrating so I'd better open it up in case something is switched on that shouldn't be. Customers hate it when they go to test a gadget and the batteries are already flat.'

I didn't want to know what was in the box, or how her customers tested the products. I certainly didn't want to know whether they were allowed to test things that they didn't buy, so I pleaded exhaustion and took myself off for another restless night. And without Eli it was nowhere near as much fun to be awake in bed.

I got up hours before I needed to, pretending that the daylight meant that it wasn't quite as appallingly early as it was. Opening my laptop, I started a spreadsheet and began to spend some of Mr King's deposit on supplies. He would never allow the traditional pink or blue balloons – his sprawling country pile was far too classy for decorations of that type – so I glanced over his budget and placed an order for some ivory tulle wrapped ones which cost about five times as much. We could save money on the linens at least. Mrs King had a selection of beautifully embroidered tablecloths that were far more expensive than I'd have been able to purchase anyway.

I phoned my florist and spent another small fortune on peach and ivory roses. Mr King had also offered to provide the champagne, but as I began to ring round caterers to find one who was willing to risk the wrath of my clients if their amuse-bouche didn't amuse enough, I also asked whether they provided additional glasses alongside the crockery.

The plans were just beginning to fall into place when the

door to my shop banged. Given that only a few people had a key, I closed my laptop and got up, hoping, though not expecting, that it might be Eli.

'You could look a bit more pleased to see me,' Lily said.

I gave her a quick hug. 'I do love you, bestie.' She hugged me back. 'I was just hoping that it might be Eli. I know, I know. He's in Paris. City of Love. Without me. Probably in danger.'

She walked past me into my kitchen and began to make me a cup of tea. 'I get it. I miss Taylor too. I tried out this new one-minute wonder gizmo that we got in at work. Not the same. Honestly, if something is worth doing, it's worth taking more than a minute and getting it right.'

I sipped my drink and tried to work out how to change the subject. 'Do you want to come and interview non-religious officiants for the naming ceremony I'm organising?'

'Are they all called Dream or River? If so, I'm in.'

'They're called Kathleen and Kara, and they both sound utterly lovely.'

'You can count on me. I love a welcome party and those non-traditional ceremonies can be so beautiful and personal. Sounds like a great idea.' She raided my cupboards until she found a packet of biscuits that Eli had somehow not discovered. 'How about we get our passports and go to Paris too?'

'No way. Not happening,' I told her.

'It's the most romantic place on Earth. It would be a work trip for you. You could pretend it's for research.'

'Eli would kill me.'

'Eli would never know. We'd just take the Eurostar, spend a couple of days mooching around the markets and seeing the Eiffel Tower. Maybe I'd bump into Taylor and we could have a quick … "chat".'

If she got Taylor alone for five minutes I didn't want to be within earshot.

'Oi, I could stay here, do my job and not fall out with my boyfriend.'

'Why are you so worried what Eli thinks all of a sudden?'

'Because whatever they do, it might be dangerous. We've lost enough people in our lives. If I deliberately put myself in harm's way he would be devastated. It's taken him years to let me close, I'm not risking it just so that we can pretend to be action stars.'

'You went on a trip with Erin, he didn't mind that.'

'It was a spa. The most dangerous part was going without sugar for two days.' I shivered at the memory. Thank goodness I'd managed to sneak in my own supply.

'Whatever. I'm going to the loo.' She set her mug on the counter, dropped her handbag on the floor and walked past me again.

I finished my tea, washed our cups and began to tidy the flat. Picking her bag up, I went to hang it on the back of a chair, missed and it hit the floor, spilling its contents including a box. A pregnancy test box. Which had been opened and presumably used.

Chapter Sixteen

If Lily wondered why I changed my mind about going to Paris she didn't mention it. Instead she shrieked and hollered and danced around my flat, tossing clothes into a bag and moaning that none of my lingerie was exciting enough to take to Paris. I tried to point out that we weren't going on a romantic break. In fact, if we caught up with Eli the only thing that would be broken would be my heart when he dumped me. I had serious misgivings, but I couldn't leave Lily to go alone to tell Taylor about the baby. That must have been what she meant by the little 'chat' she wanted to have. It didn't sound little to me, but I was glad she wasn't as nervous about it as I felt on her behalf.

She nipped home whilst I finished closing up the shop and arrived back within the hour, dragging a pink suitcase on wheels that was so small she might as well have picked it up and carried it. Though that would have limited her ability to take out our fellow commuters' ankles on the way to the station. If she was granting herself points for damage caused, she would have been on the way to a grand prize. As it was, we reached the Eurostar station with only minor injuries to passers-by, handed over our passports and an obscene amount of money and were treated to the two last seats in a full carriage. Nothing, though, could dampen Lily's enthusiasm.

I didn't know how Lily could be so cheerful. I couldn't have stayed so calm if I'd been travelling to tell Eli that we were expecting. I'd have been so nervous I'd have been chewing my nails and struggling to sit still. Lily, though, was reclining in her seat on board the Eurostar train, as only she could because even I at my not-great-height couldn't have spread out as much as she was. One fellow, dressed in a pin-striped suit and carrying a black umbrella, despite the warm weather, glared at me as he took his seat. He was probably one of Lily's victims, given the way he rubbed his calf as he settled himself into a chair. But at that moment Lily sat forward, and he saw her and the vest top that was struggling to cover her cleavage and began to offer an oily smile in our direction instead. I ignored him, wishing that this journey was more like the underground where no-one made eye contact, let alone spoke to each other.

'All we need now is some champagne and this would be perfect.'

I stared at her. 'Do you think that would be a good idea?'

'You're right. Coffee first. We can have a drink when we get there. It won't be so expensive.'

Maybe she was in denial. I wondered if I should have asked her outright how far along she was and what she wanted to do, but I realised that I had to trust her to tell me when she was ready. Besides, she had every right to want to tell the father before she talked to me. She knew I'd support her no matter what. I could only hope that Taylor would do the same. I picked up my handbag from under my seat and set out for the buffet car. Halfway there I realised that, although coffee wasn't as prohibited as alcohol for Lily, it probably still wasn't good for her to have too much in her condition. Scanning the menu, I tried and failed to work out what she ought to be having. In lieu of any sensible decisions I bought her a bottle of sparkling water and myself a posh orange juice.

Rolling with the motion of the train as I walked back to my seat, I squeezed past the queue outside the loo, dodged past the toddlers who were running screaming away from their mothers and made it back to my seat. I was beginning to wish that I had gone for the wine. I went to offer Lily the water, but she took the juice and thanked me. 'How did you know I was craving something sweet? It's so hot on here and the kids have been driving me crazy. Who knew how loud small children were?'

Lily crossed her legs and sat back, sipping her drink with her eyes closed. By contrast I found myself unable to relax. If Lily had no idea how much hard work it was to look after children, how was she going to cope? Especially as Taylor's job was similar to Eli's, including spells where they disappeared off at short notice on mysterious missions and we often wouldn't know where they were or when they would be back.

I pulled out my mobile and began searching for parenting advice websites. If Lily wasn't going to read up, then it looked like it might be up to me to help her.

'Ooh, are you reading up on where we should go?' Lily asked, opening her eyes.

I stared at her. She shrugged and tried to go back to sleep again. I continued to read. A little while later we reached the beginning of the tunnel. My phone reception cut out and I had to decide whether to pay a small fortune to access the on-board wi-fi, or whether to take a few minutes to get my head around everything that I had already read. Deep in a sea of information about labour and breastfeeding, I decided that I'd read enough. Once Lily was ready to start talking about what she wanted to do, I'd be well prepared.

The warmth of the cabin and the dimmed lights outside soothed me, despite the turbulence in my tummy, and I closed my eyes as Lily had done. I woke up to bright sunshine. We had crossed the Channel and were hurtling towards Paris.

'Bonjour,' Lily greeted me.

I blinked, stretched and sat up. 'What time is it?'

'Time to grab our bags, check in to our hotel and do some shopping.'

I wondered when she was planning to meet up with Taylor and tell him about the baby, but then I realised that this would mean running the risk of Eli seeing me here. He had been in enough stressful situations that he wouldn't want me anywhere near this. I began to kick myself again that I'd let

Lily talk me into coming with her, but she had been my best friend for years. I couldn't leave her to travel here by herself to tell Taylor. I looked at her, trying to reach her bag on the overhead shelf and failing, then giggling and flirting with the guard who helped her to carry it down, and wondered how on earth we had ended up in this situation. She was usually so careful to have safe sex, as she was only too keen to tell me about, in often excruciating yet educational detail. I was amazed that she wasn't as freaked out as I felt about being here to break the big news.

Where London had been warm, Paris was positively baking. For once I envied Lily's wardrobe choices of a tiny pair of shorts and a vest top. I wouldn't be able to borrow them though. On Lily they were short enough, more like hot pants. On me they would have barely passed as knickers. When we joined the queue to get a taxi, we found ourselves with five men arguing over who got to drive us. Not one of them looked at me. I didn't mind. I was grungy from the journey and looking forward to a shower.

I was daydreaming of a beautiful boutique hotel, with wooden shutters and a view of the Eiffel Tower, when our taxi drew up outside a fairly nondescript concrete block of a building. I got out nervously, glancing around to make sure that Eli hadn't mysteriously appeared to spot us. I still hadn't worked out how I was going to explain to him that we'd come, and just had to hope that once he heard why Lily needed to see Taylor that he would understand.

'I'm guessing we don't have a swimming pool?' I asked with a sigh.

'It was cheap, and available at the last minute, but it does have air conditioning and a bath.'

'I'm sold. Let's check in.'

The driver carried Lily's bag to the door, leaving me to carry my own. He hung around for a minute in a cloud of his own body odour, but as Lily swished off to the stairs with the key to our room, he realised that she wasn't going to give him her number, let alone invite him in, and he disappeared off with only the sound of his car horn making clear his frustration at having struck out.

To save a bit more cash Lily and I were sharing a twin room. Lily must have gone for a wander whilst I was showering because I re-emerged, towel wrapped around my hair, to find bottles of cold juice and giant bags of crisps on the bedside table.

'I got the munchies,' she explained. 'I asked where the nearest shop was but there was a sweet guy behind the bar who gave me some of his own stash.' She had changed into a black lace vest top, neon pink bra and black mini skirt, paired with some cornflower-blue stilettos that matched her eyes. It was going to be interesting to see what her take on a maternity wardrobe was going to be, not that she had any sign of a bump yet. If I hadn't seen the test box in her bag I'd never have guessed, and I wondered briefly whether she would be put out once she had a big belly and men suddenly stopped being so helpful to her. But then she handed me a drink and smiled, and I realised people wouldn't stop being nice as she was so effortlessly upbeat that she would draw kindness to her regardless. I hugged her, and she squeezed me back. 'This trip is going to beat any fancy spa,' she told me.

I tensed yet again. 'That was work,' I assured her. 'And it wasn't much fun. There was no decent food for a start.'

'Plus, you had to go with Erin.' She shuddered.

'Actually, I'm starting to mellow. Maybe the aromatherapy oils there worked after all. I mean, I'm still angry about the whole doping Ben up and sneaking him onto a ferry, but she's not quite as evil as I thought she was. She does genuinely love my brother.'

Lily picked up a glass and handed it to me. 'Well, here's to Paris, city of romance, my best friend and to having a good time. The boys are going to be so glad that we've come to help.'

Chapter Seventeen

'*Help*?' I shrieked. 'No, not help. Talk maybe, but definitely not help. Lily, Eli will go mental if he thinks we came to interfere.'

She pouted. 'You helped them when Erin asked you.'

'Not by choice.' My voice was so squeaky now that only bats and dogs would be able to hear it easily. 'Besides, that was finding someone at a spa. The only dangerous part was trying to cope without bread or pasta. This is totally different.'

Lily seemed strangely keen to do anything other than find Taylor and explain about the pregnancy, but if I were in her shoes I'd probably have felt the same way, and so I tried to be as understanding as I could. 'You need a shopping trip,' she diagnosed. 'We're only five minutes from the Moulin Rouge. There's a shop around the corner that is famous for selling the most enormous latex ...'

I stuck my fingers in my ears so that I couldn't hear and didn't take them out until she tapped me on the shoulder and spoke again. 'We'll call it research. You never know, we might come across something useful for your shop.'

'Doubtful ...' I began, but then Lily reminded me of the time we'd flogged a load of naughty teddy bears, complete with furry boners and lacy underwear to one of my hardest-to-please clients. 'Though it would be useful to have a few gift possibilities up my sleeve. I fear this naming ceremony, if it goes well, will have Mr King coming back every birthday and Christmas and, quite frankly, I'm out of ideas. But I'm coming back before it gets dark and I am not going into any clubs.'

Lily mistook my reluctant acceptance for excitement and dragged me down the street in search of some new products that hadn't yet crossed the Channel, most likely because no-one else would dare bring them through customs. I wished that I'd worn clothes that covered more of me; my own cotton navy-blue skirt and white lace top had felt like comfortable summer chic earlier, but when faced with the customers of the shop that we were in, I wanted to be covered from my ankles to my neck. Lily used to assure me that it was perfectly normal to go into adult shops and that I should try not to look so embarrassed or shifty myself, but then the place that she managed felt like it had been cleaned at some point in the last decade. This one looked as though it could use a good wipe and some disinfectant, but I wasn't going to volunteer.

I was tempted to close my eyes so that I didn't have to see any of the merchandise, but I was scared of what would happen if I let my guard down. It must have offended even Lily's fairly relaxed sensibilities as we left empty-handed. 'Time to go? Maybe treat ourselves to a crepe?' I suggested.

'Just one more,' Lily begged. 'We didn't check out the place that my friend told me about yet.'

I wasn't sure how this research trip was going to lead into Lily's plan to talk to Taylor, but it was sure to keep us in places where we weren't likely to bump into Eli by accident, so I followed her.

'So, when are you going to talk to Taylor?' I asked, as I dodged the shifty looking man smoking a roll-up outside the shop. I took a second deep inhale when I realised that he wasn't smoking the traditional gitane, but something entirely more herbal. Perhaps if I breathed deeply enough I'd be able to follow Lily in without panicking.

'Maybe I'll buy him a little something,' Lily mused, running her hands through the racks of barely-there underwear.

'Don't you have enough to share with him already?'

Lily shot me a glance. 'I'm going downstairs to look at their specialty items.' I stayed where I was.

The walls were lined with DVD boxes. I couldn't understand most of the titles, but I assumed that they followed the terrible pun style that Lily's shop favoured. If this was the tame stock then I had no wish to see what kind of items my friend was currently viewing. Still, I needed to kill some time while Lily was busy and Eli might have appreciated some of the lingerie so I had a quick look, given that I was there, but it didn't leave quite enough to the imagination for me. Indeed, it lacked so much coverage or support I could hardly see the point, though Lily had tried to tell me many times that you only wore clothes like these when you didn't plan to have them on for long. I preferred the romantic items that my shop at home sold, that felt smooth under your fingers and invited you to feel good, rather than chilly, in them.

The shop-keeper must have finished his spliff, as he opened the door and entered the room, lifting the counter so that he could go and sit behind it. Lily said that part of the reason that she was so good at her job was because she was unshockable, so she was able to fix her customers up with whatever suited their needs. Also, she had a natural curiosity that had her seeking out new items, as we were currently, and approachability so that she didn't scare off the more timid customer. This man was sorely lacking in that department. Where Lily greeted her customers with a smile, he did so with a scowl, as if he disapproved of anyone who came to shop there. I began to wonder how he stayed in business, until he scowled at me with an increased glower and I found myself picking up several items which I had no intention of ever using and carrying them to the till to pay just to try and cheer him up a bit. I just hoped that the carrier bags were going to be labelled discreetly as I didn't want anyone on the street to see where I'd been.

'Did you get something for Eli?' Lily asked, hefting a full metal basket onto the counter.

‘Not as much as you seem to have found,’ I remarked.

‘I was hoping that if I bought enough, I’d be able to claim this as a work trip and get some expenses back.’

If anyone else had said that I’d have assumed that they were joking, but Lily was fearless and might just be able to convince her manager. We emerged from the gloom of the shop, blinking in the sunshine. I felt like a lizard, warming my blood in the sun after the cool darkness of the shop.

‘That was fun. I think I need a coffee to celebrate though, it was like a crypt in their basement,’ Lily said. Given that she sometimes appeared to be almost nocturnal herself and drawn to the darkness, it must have been pretty extreme down there.

I agreed with her, partly because I needed something to pick me up, and partly because I wanted the excuse to get just a little further away from the shop. Besides, one coffee couldn’t hurt; we hadn’t had any on the train, and we were in Paris. It was practically a requirement that we sit outside at a café and enjoy the warmth of the day. ‘Okay,’ I said, ‘but after that we really need to think about what you’re going to tell Taylor.’

She shrugged and tapped her bulging pile of bags. ‘I think I can win him around.’ I wasn’t sure that a ton of kinky junk would take his mind off the fact that he was going to have a baby, but if Lily thought it would help to soften the news, who was I to argue?

Chapter Eighteen

'Are you sure you don't want to go out?' Lily asked as she swept past me, marching down the hotel corridor.

I stared at her as she teetered along on her five-inch heels. Surely pregnant women were supposed to slow down? She ought to be feeling too nauseous to be bugging me to go clubbing. I hustled to keep up. 'We're not even supposed to be here. I only agreed to come with you because of the test,' I told her.

'What are you talking about? I thought it would be nice for us to come and spend some time together. We're so busy these days, you with Eli, me with Taylor, when was the last time that we just hung out?'

'We just got back from holiday. We spent two weeks doing nothing but hanging out.'

'I want to spend some time with you, having fun.' She pouted. Was she upset because once the baby came it would get harder for her to go out as she was used to doing? I tried to be sympathetic, but it was hard as she didn't show any of the same nerves that I did about the guys being upset when they found out that we were here. I wanted her to see Taylor, tell him her news, and then get ourselves back home again before we interrupted their work. She didn't seem to share my reticence.

'One evening out? I'll even let you choose the club, though it would be far more fun if you let me choose.'

'We're not here to have fun,' I pointed out.

'I'm not going to spend the evening sat in our room watching crap TV that I can't understand. I just wanted us to have an adventure, like we used to, before you got all coupled up and traded me in for your psycho sister-in-law,' she announced, stomping past me. My own shoes barely had a two-inch heel and I couldn't walk as quickly as she could.

I followed her to the bar in our hotel and watched as she

ordered us a bottle of white wine. 'What are you doing? You shouldn't be drinking.'

'When did you start worrying so much about what I should and shouldn't be doing?' she snapped. I reached past her for the bottle on the counter, poured myself a glass before I dared to let myself reply. 'I didn't mean that, Daisy. I'm sorry.'

We sat at the counter, side by side, in silence, our backs to the room. It was no hardship, though the room lacked the warmth and comfort of a decent pub. Tomorrow morning the same tables would be set for breakfast, but for now it was convenient, the wine was cold and I could try and get to the bottom of what on earth was going on with my friend.

I downed my drink but was relieved that Lily merely sipped at hers. I didn't want to pick another fight, but it wasn't easy to watch her not looking after the baby. Eventually, when I'd drunk most of the bottle and was feeling just a little woozy, I couldn't keep my mouth shut any longer. 'What are you going to do exactly? We're going to have to break the news to them somehow, they're going to be furious if they find out that we're here otherwise.'

'I thought they might be glad of the help, just like they were when you and Erin helped them out.'

Was she jealous that I'd had to spend time locked away with my brother's kidnapper-come-girlfriend? 'I told you, that was work. I don't make a habit out of living on salad leaves and having to fake sex addictions.' It was probably for the best that I didn't go into detail about the whisky and pizza, not to mention the sneaky time with Eli in the massage room. She'd never have believed that it was all work.

I wanted to ask the bartender if they sold any chips. I needed something to soak up the booze but he was either put off from interacting with us by the tension, or he was scared that he would be fired if he didn't keep every glass polished to perfection, as he steadfastly kept his back to us and continued wiping as we drank.

Lily poured herself another glass before tipping the dregs of the bottle into mine. 'So, they won't be pleased that we're here?' she muttered. I turned to stare at her. She shrugged. 'I wanted to be helpful.'

'Lily, they'd be fuming. Haven't you seen how tired they are when they get back from trips like this? Eli always returns with bags under his eyes like he hasn't slept for a week. He loses weight, has bad dreams. Why would they ever risk us if they could help it?' To her credit, Lily finally seemed to take in what I was saying. The anger and jealousy faded, and she looked even more tiny than normal, sat in her mini skirt and vest top, balanced precariously on a metal bar stool so high that her feet couldn't reach the ground.

'I love you, Lily,'

'I love you too'

'But I wouldn't risk my relationship with Eli to come and have a jolly here. He means too much to me. And I'm sorry if you were upset that I had to go away with Erin and not you, but Eli and I have lost too much time arguing in the past, I wouldn't risk our being together now by deliberately doing something that would upset him so much. I wouldn't have come at all, but I didn't want you to have to tell Taylor about the baby by yourself.'

'Baby?'

'You don't need to hide it from me. I saw the test in your bag, and then you wanted to come here to see them. I came so that you didn't have to tell Taylor on your own. I know you must be scared, that's why I'm here.'

'Daisy …' she at least had the decency to look downcast as she broke the news to me. 'There's no baby. There never was. I just wanted to change my pill but as my periods aren't that regular the doctor made me take a test first. I came here because I wanted to have what you and Erin had. I wanted to have another adventure with you.'

I exploded from my seat, until either my brain wobbled

or the floor did, and I collapsed back down again. 'No baby? You risked my relationship with Eli just because you were jealous? Do you have any idea of how selfish that was? He's going to be fuming. I'll be lucky if he even gives me a chance to explain why we're here before he dumps me and breaks my heart again.' My voice rose even louder and now the bartender stopped polishing glasses and just legged it out from behind the bar and into the staff room, closing the door behind him and giving no sign that he was ever going to come back. 'I lost ten years with Eli because we were bickering and weren't ready to let ourselves try and be together. We just got past it, and it's hard because we both have so much baggage. We've lost people so close to us that it's been a long road for him to accept how much I love him, and I do, with everything that I have. He's my best friend.'

'I thought I was your best friend,' she muttered, and she stuck her bottom lip out in a pose I hadn't seen since Ben was a teenager and Dad caught him hacking a US television network trying to fake emails and commission a new series of *Firefly*.

'You are too, but he's my future, Lily. And I wouldn't risk that for anything stupid like a weekend in Paris playing at being James Bond. This is their job. They don't need our help, and they don't want it. They want us back home, safe, and not doing anything that could jeopardise people's lives. This isn't a game. I want to spend the rest of my life with Eli, and that isn't going to happen if he thinks that I'm a silly little kid who needs to follow him around to get attention. I knew it was a risk coming here, but I genuinely believed that you were pregnant and needed my support. If I'd known that this was a petty display of jealousy I would never have come. Now, I'm going back to my room to pack, then I'm leaving before Eli finds out I was here and dumps me. Because if he breaks up with me over this, I swear I'll never forgive you.'

'I'd say it was a little too late for that,' said a voice behind me.

Chapter Nineteen

'Daisy, open the door,' Eli called, as he knocked yet again. 'Daisy,' he called again. 'I'm going to count to ten, then I'm coming in.'

I ignored him, assuming that if he had to go and track down a member of staff and talk them into lending him the spare key that I'd have time to wash my face and pull myself together before he saw me. I hadn't counted on his super spy lock picking skills though, and a moment later he was next to me in the bedroom, looking at me with concern. The relief was palpable. I'd expected anger. But not red-hot anger, not the type Eli would use to help him take apart someone dangerous. I'd been expecting a coldness, borne of disappointment and regret, that would have him walk away because I'd betrayed his trust.

'You're talking to me?' I asked, even though it was obvious that he was. He took a bottle of water from the mini fridge, twisted the cap and took a long drink before passing it to me. The wine I'd drunk sat heavy and acidic in my tummy, so I finished what was left.

The air conditioning had been turned off when we went out and as I stood there the air was thick with humidity and tension. Eli took a seat on my bed, the springs complaining at how hard he dropped down. Anytime I had dared to picture how he would feel when he discovered that we were here too, it never ended well, but now he mostly looked at a loss for what to say. The most that I had dared to wish for was that he was understanding once he learnt about the baby. But there was no baby. I'd seen the box, jumped to conclusions and now we were here, where we shouldn't have been, because Lily had been jealous.

My head was beginning to throb. Stepping back, my legs

hit the edge of the bed and I sank onto it too. Eli reached for me, and suddenly, I wasn't thinking about anything anymore, except for how it felt as we lay together.

And after we had made love, I rested my head on his chest, listening to the slow beat of his heart. By contrast mine was still hammering. I could tell he wasn't asleep; his breathing was still silent, lacking the slight rasp that came when he was in a deep sleep. I kissed his shoulder and waited for him to speak.

He didn't. Eventually I couldn't hold it in any longer. 'Are you angry?'

The daylight had faded to dusk, just light enough to make out shadows, but not enough to see Eli's face clearly. I could picture it though, as he weighed up his feelings carefully before choosing his words.

'I can't say I was pleased that you were here. When I spotted you at the bar, I was seconds away from asking what the hell you were thinking.'

My pulse rate picked up even more. Beneath my cheek Eli's hadn't changed, and I wondered whether it was this ability to stay calm under pressure that made it possible for him to do his job. 'How much did you hear of our argument?'

'Enough to realise that you hadn't made the decision to come here lightly, and though I'd rather that you weren't here at all, I understand that you came to support your friend.'

'So, you're not feeling smug because you heard me announce to everyone within earshot how much I love you?'

His chest shook as he laughed. 'That may have helped too.' He kissed the top of my head. I wondered whether there was a small part of him that was gloating that I had made such a public declaration in front of Taylor.

He grew still again. 'I don't find it easy to talk about my feelings, so I may not have stood up and declared to anyone within earshot, that I love you, but I do. When my mum died, it hurt so much that I didn't ever want to love someone so much that I could risk being that broken again, so if I get over-protective, you have to understand why.'

'I do,' I assured him.

'Were you really scared of how I'd react? Because I would hate that. I don't ever want you to be scared of me. I didn't think you were until I saw you run out when I arrived.'

I nudged him with my elbow. 'You might be big, but I'm not afraid of you.' He chuckled and drew me against him again. 'Afraid of losing you, yes. Mostly I was just drunk on too much cheap wine and far too much anger myself. I felt like Lily tricked me and risked our relationship. I should have asked her outright, not assumed when I saw the test, but she seemed so keen to see Taylor I thought it meant that she needed to tell him first. Now I'm fuming that she was willing to come, even though she knew I didn't want to, just so we could pretend to be having an adventure together again. I hate being angry. It destroys me inside that I feel this way about such a good friend.' I reached down and entwined my fingers with his. 'You're not the only one who is scared of losing someone you love. I promised I wouldn't do anything dangerous, but by being in the same hotel as you I think we probably did. I could imagine you turning and walking away, and I'm not sure I could cope with that.' Even just thinking about it was hard, and I found myself beginning to well up. Letting go of his hand so that I could wipe my eyes, I tried to hide how emotional I was, but Eli could tell.

'It's okay,' he assured me. 'We're fine, though I almost lost it when you announced that we were off doing James Bond stuff.' I groaned. 'Don't worry, there was no-one else nearby. Taylor checked out the situation as soon as we saw you both.'

'I have no idea how Lily managed to book us into the same place. What was she thinking?'

'It's Lily, who knows? Maybe Taylor told her where we'd be before he left.'

'She said she wanted us to have an adventure together. Have I been an awful friend? I never meant to ignore her once we got together. I don't understand why she would do something this stupid.'

'Maybe she didn't realise how angry you would be? Lily would never mean to hurt you. I guess she just heard us talking about Paris and got carried away with her daydreams. She doesn't know how anxious I get about keeping you safe.'

I kissed his cheek, grateful that he was so understanding, even if I wasn't ready to be so understanding myself. 'Did you manage to solve the problem that brought you over?'

'We're no closer to finding out why Jean-Luc left, if that's what you mean. There's no sign that he left in a hurry, suggesting that whatever happened, he had time to think it through.'

'Isn't that a good thing? It means he didn't run away?'

'Or maybe he knew what was going to happen because he helped to cause it and ran before we could catch him.'

'When you put it like that ...'

Chapter Twenty

It was nice to be home again. Familiar. It should have been comforting, but I knew something was missing. Lily. I had been back for three days and I hadn't yet replied to any of her texts. 'Have you seen Lily since you got home?' Dad asked, handing me a cup of tea. I shook my head. He and Cody exchanged looks. It was strange to see my dad forming a strong enough relationship with her that they could talk without saying a word, and yet at the same time I was really pleased that he had managed to heal himself enough that it was possible.

'I will. I've just been busy.'

He knew I was bluffing. No-one wanted to buy romantic gifts in the summer. It felt like I'd brought the sunshine home from Paris with me. It was too hot and sticky to have romantic thoughts. All anyone wanted to do was to sit still in the shade with a cool drink. No-one made any trips that they didn't need to. The underground was so boiling that staff were handing out free bottles of water. My temper had been as high as the temperature.

Lily and I had never had a serious argument before, and neither of us knew how to handle it. Lily had sent a couple of messages, not saying much, just letting me know that she had my shoes and a lipstick. I knew I ought to write back but wasn't quite ready. Lily frequently worked late into the night, often my lunch-break was at the same time as her breakfast, and it felt odd to eat alone, but not so strange that I felt ready to call her yet.

'Did Lily actually tell you that she was pregnant?' Cody asked.

I shook my head. 'No, and I know that I'm being unreasonable. It's not like she lied to me explicitly. But she was still reckless. I went with her because I thought she needed me. She knew Eli would be upset if we interfered with their work, and she wanted me to go just because she was jealous of the time I spent with Erin.'

'And was Eli angry with you?' Dad tossed the dressing into the salad and brought it over to the table, alongside a loaf of fresh bread. I went to tear a piece off and burnt the tips of my fingers.

'Careful,' Dad said, a minute too late. 'It's fresh out of the oven.'

'He would have been, but he heard me shouting at Lily and realised what had happened. He's got this weird preoccupation with me never going near his work out of fear of losing me.'

'Sounds rational to me,' my dad said. 'I can understand not wanting to risk people I love ever again. I'm just glad Ben is stuck behind a keyboard in the office if I'm honest.'

Cody brought her own drink and sat next to me at the table. 'What is it that is really bothering you?' she asked. 'You and Lily are so close. It doesn't seem like you to fall out like this. Especially because, as you say, she may have been a little negligent, but she wasn't actually dishonest. She didn't know you only agreed to go because you saw the pregnancy test. She must have thought that you wanted to go on the trip as much as she did.'

'She booked us into the same hotel as them. She did know that I was nervous of bumping into Eli. He wanted to protect me, keep me safe, not have me end up right in the middle of his trip.'

I answered, somewhat petulantly to be honest. I didn't go full teenager and pout as I said it, but Dad could tell I wasn't happy. Cody must have been able to tell as she fixed me with a direct gaze as she spoke again.

'What is it that has you upset really?'

'It's not as though Lily has been a paragon of sense since

you've known her. It can't really have shocked you that she would want to get involved,' Dad pointed out.

Cody must have seen my discomfort, because she took the bowl of salad from my hands, set it on the table and drew me in for a hug. I wasn't expecting to, but I found myself becoming emotional at the contact. Was this how it felt to be soothed by a mum? I could hardly remember my own mum holding me. Eli's mum had been generous in her affections, and being safe in Cody's arms just reminded me of how much I missed her too. Then there was no holding back the tears.

'I could have lost him, Cody,' I choked out between sobs. 'I'm angry with myself, because I jumped to conclusions about the pregnancy test and put myself in a position that I knew might upset him. And I can't lose him. I love him so much, and I don't want to lose anyone else. I'm so scared.' Cody held me as I sobbed. It wasn't that delicate crying either, my shoulders were shaking and I could barely draw a breath.

'It's okay, you haven't lost him,' Cody whispered, over and over again into my ear until I got my breathing under control. Then she passed me a tissue and kept holding my hand as I talked. It should have felt strange to be sat there, holding onto another grown woman whilst my dad stood there looking slightly out of his depth watching us, but it didn't. It felt nice to be safe and loved. Finally, I managed to pull myself together enough to speak.

'Luckily, he overheard me telling Lily how much I love him and that I would never have risked our relationship lightly, but he's as screwed up as I am. I hate to think of what he has to do when he goes away for work. He never tells me much of what he's been up to. I know that he wants to protect me from that. It's hard enough for me to let him go, and I have you, Dad and Ben. I know he's scared, I am too, but I don't know how to help him handle that fear. It's not a sexist, protective thing. My goodness, his boss is the most incredible, formidable woman. Sometimes I think we're just both so messed up by our grief that we risk letting it get in the way of our relationship.'

'It is hard to let go of pain, or even just to learn to live with it and despite it, but if you can be brave and let yourself try, you might be surprised at how much joy you can still find.' Cody turned to beam at my dad. I wondered how much she was thinking about the breakdown that had led to her leaving her successful career as a photo-journalist and to her new life here with her gallery.

'I should have set a better example too,' Dad continued.

'You did the best you could,' I reassured him. 'Ben and I never went hungry. We knew that you loved us.'

'I was so devastated when your mum died that I forgot for a long time that she would have wanted me to keep having fun and stretching myself, otherwise it would have been as though her death took both of us. I should have tried harder to make sure that you and Ben were happy.'

'We were,' I began, but he waved his hand to stop my protests.

'Eli too, after Grace died. I knew he was struggling but I had nothing left to give. The grief was so heavy, it felt like I could barely move, barely even think.' Cody let go of my hand and got up to fuss over my Dad instead. It was lovely to see him being looked after, cared for. He'd done his best over the years, and it hadn't been easy, bringing me and Ben up on his own. I was glad to see he wasn't lonely anymore. Maybe it was easier to see him holding another woman because I barely remembered him holding my mum, but they looked good together. Happy. He was wearing one of his old cotton shirts and beige trousers, but he had paired it with a rainbow-coloured waistcoat which left the entire outfit altogether less drab than it would have been before he met Cody. For her part, Cody was wearing a purple silk kimono over a pair of yellow yoga pants. She truly did brighten up any room that she was in, and not just due to her clothes. She kissed his cheek and he smiled at her.

Dad made a suggestion. 'It seems to me that you and Eli are fine, wary obviously, but fine. So why don't you call Lily? I'm making my famous burritos.' Dad had never made the dish before, but if he was confident that it was going to be good then I wasn't going to argue with him. His palate had come back, along with his fashion skills, however eclectic they may be, when he had met Cody.

'I'll call Lily,' I promised.

'Do you have any appointments this afternoon? Why don't you walk over to her shop and invite her for dinner?'

Chapter Twenty-One

There are not many dads who would encourage their daughters to go to a sex shop, but I had to admit that it was a good idea. Lily drew me in for such a big hug that she had to shout at a couple of her clients to stop perving on us and go back to buying items so that they could go be kinky in the privacy of their own homes.

By the time I brought her home Eli had also managed to forget that he had been cross with Lily. He greeted her with a grin that made me wonder why I had ever been so worried. Unless something else was going on? He handed her a glass of wine as we sat down to eat. 'Did Taylor make it home yet?' he asked.

I was about to set a dish of grated cheese on the table, but I paused. 'What do you mean?' I should have realised straight away that Taylor was missing; goodness knows that he was enormous and having him absent gave us half the space back in the kitchen.

'He got held up at customs,' Eli explained. 'The Boss was fuming, she's been phoning me to check in every day since we found her. Honestly, it's a good job she's already at the retreat because if she didn't need stress relief before then she certainly did after this. We're supposed to keep a low profile, especially on trips like last weekend where we'd been hoping to slip in and out of France without Jean-Luc or any of his team knowing that we had been there. We still don't know why he's here and who might be behind whatever is going on.'

'It was my fault,' Lily said, staring down at her plate. 'Taylor was carrying my suitcase.' I pictured the man mountain pulling the tiny pink case behind him. 'Apparently they pulled him over in customs.' I was surprised. In all my years of travelling, I'd never actually seen someone pulled out of a line before to be searched. Maybe it was his height, or maybe they could sense his secret skills. Lily took a sip of her wine before she continued. 'So, the customs official makes him open his bag, and it starts buzzing. He said they thought they were going to have to evacuate until he convinced them it was safe to look. They asked if he packed it himself, and he said yes because you know you're supposed to, so they asked him what was making the noise and he couldn't tell them. It was a new gadget I found in that shop I took Daisy to. They couldn't find the off switch, it took them half an hour to get it to stop vibrating.' She shook her head. 'I really hope I get it back.'

Eli by now was howling with laughter. He opened the fridge, drew out a bottle of prosecco and popped the cork. 'Anyone for a drink?'

Lily ignored him. 'Taylor was trying to be kind. He spent most of the day in a cell, thanks to me. They called his office to vouch for him, and apparently he had to explain what had happened and what he had been caught with.'

'Is he back home again?' Dad asked, ignoring Eli's fit of not so silent giggles.

Eli could barely keep a straight face but just about managed to tell us the rest. 'He is, but he got an earful, including the new deputy manager shouting something about not wanting to see his face for a few days so he's been working from home. He decided not to come until this had blown over a bit.' Watching Eli double over now as he laughed, I thought that Taylor was being a little optimistic if he thought that Eli would be letting go of this soon, or ever. Dad shot him a look and eventually he got himself under control and came to join us at the table.

'It was pretty funny,' Erin admitted, as Dad handed her a loaded plate. Ben dug into his food without looking up. I wasn't sure if he hadn't found it funny or hadn't noticed that anyone was missing.

I wanted to ask if there was any more news about Jean-Luc, but Eli was looking so relaxed that I didn't want to lose that by making him think about work again. We sat at the table together and ate, teasing Lily about her customers, Dad about his new penchant for tie-dyed clothes and Eli about his fondness for not wearing anything cheery, as he was currently in yet another plain black suit and shirt. Even if he did look lick-your-lips gorgeous in it.

It felt good, to be there in a room full of people that I loved. Even having Erin there wasn't too bad. I had a little more of the wine than normal, celebrating my newly hatched plan of not being so scared, and tried hard to enjoy the people around me without wondering how I would manage if anything were to happen to them.

My positivity lasted through the tipsy trip downstairs where Eli ended up putting me over his shoulder and carrying me to bed. It certainly lasted through what we did when we got there. It had faded a little when I woke up the next morning to find my head thumping, and disappeared entirely when I realised that whilst the pain was real, the banging was actually coming from my front door.

I pulled the sheet back up to cover me, but it was too thin to cut any of the noise. Eventually Eli tugged the covers from my grip. 'Are you going to get that?'

'Wasn't planning to.' I didn't open my eyes as I spoke.

He laughed and got up, reaching for his pants and T-shirt. Both black. Thankfully so was the coffee that he brought me back, along with paracetamol and a couple of slices of toast. 'I showed him into your shop and told him that you'd be there in ten minutes. If you're quick you might be able to sneak in a shower.'

I groaned, but business was business, and I made a point always to help people find romance whenever I could. Grabbing my dressing-gown, I tried to sneak around the corner from my room and into the cloakroom that passed as a bathroom. Pulling my hair into a messy ponytail, I kicked myself for forgetting to bring clean clothes in with me, and instead had to make do with the trousers and T-shirt that I'd left hanging on the back of the door from earlier in the week that hadn't yet made it as far as the laundry basket. Brushing my teeth made me feel better, but I had to hope that this would be a straightforward sale as I didn't have the energy to deal with anything complicated.

No such luck. I opened the bathroom door and crossed the three steps that took me into my shop. There, sat ramrod straight at the counter and drinking a coffee that Eli must have made, was Mr King.

'Good morning. I apologise for the impromptu visit.'

It wasn't like him to apologise for anything. Maybe I was so hungover I'd missed something important. If only the shower and caffeine had woken me up a little more. Though likely I'd never have felt ready for a visit from Mr King. I stood there, waiting for him to explain. Eventually he spoke again. 'I know you offered to liaise with those caterers you mentioned but I wanted to use the firm my wife uses for her dinner parties, well, they've telephoned her this morning. They've got a nasty sickness bug going round. Apparently even though we still have four days to go, they can't guarantee that they'll all be clear of it by then and they don't dare to take any risks in case I'd sue. Ought to take the buggers to court for wimping out, what do you say?'

I didn't dare say a word. Mr King took some managing at the best of times, but now, hungover and on the back foot, I certainly wasn't at my finest.

'I was just wondering whether I could prevail upon you to do some additional organising?'

I couldn't guarantee that I was going to be able to keep my breakfast down, let alone plan further ahead than that, but then he added a few more crucial words. 'I'll pay for your time, of course.'

'I'm sure I'll be able to arrange something,' I told him, wondering just what I was going to be able to conjure up at such short notice.

Chapter Twenty-Two

'It's no good. I've phoned everyone I can think of and they're all busy. At this rate I'll be hiring the guy who smokes whilst he's serving from the greasy spoon café to serve us all sausage and chips. And then Mr King will fire me. Worse, he'll shout at me, a lot, and then fire me. And he'll tell his rich friends and I'll lose all my clients,' I wailed.

Lily took pity on me, handed me yet another cup of tea and some more paracetamol and locked the door to my shop. 'You're not expecting anyone else in today, I checked the diary. I'm giving you a day off.'

'I don't need a day off,' I said, but I still followed her up the stairs to my dad's flat. 'I need a miracle. Preferably one who can cook.'

Lily sat me down at the table and raided Dad's fridge. Finding a bowl of leftover spicy bean stew, she called out 'success!' She stuck it into the microwave, pressed a few buttons and once it beeped, she served it to me with a chunk of homemade bread and a fork. 'Eat that, then you can sleep for an hour. I'll wake you up before I leave for work and we'll fix this.'

I dragged the fork from bowl to mouth, thinking as I did that Lily was crazy to suggest that I'd ever feel well enough to come up with a plan that would satisfy the famously pernickety Mr King, and yet, surprisingly, as I ate I realised I was slowly beginning to feel better. And once the bowl was empty, I knew that Lily was right again, as my eyes felt heavy. I let her guide me to the sofa in Dad's living room. He'd spent so many lonely years in here before he met Cody that his scent had permeated into the furniture, and now it comforted me as Lily covered me with a blanket and told me to sleep.

'Thank you,' I whispered, as I closed my eyes. 'I don't know what I'd do without you.'

‘You wouldn’t have ended up getting into a pickle in Paris,’ she said, but then she laughed to show that I was forgiven for my reaction and left me to sleep. When I woke up again, my headache was all gone, my stomach felt more settled, despite the spicy meal, and I sat up, blinking and stretching. Lily was still there and promptly handed me a pad of paper and a pen. ‘I’ve got to go, we’ve got a shipment of pheromone sprays coming in shortly and if I don’t get there soon Steve is likely to open them and try to test them on himself. Last time they made him smell like a decomposed badger, but he thought he was irresistible. He scared off at least a dozen customers before I sent him home to wash. Goodness only knows what the people on the tube made of him. I can just picture him, smiling at girls thinking he was tempting them when really they were just trying not to be ill.’

‘Thanks for all the images there, Lily,’ I said, feeling very relieved that my stomach was more settled. Otherwise I really would have lost it. Steve thought that, as the owner, it was his duty to test new products as they came in, and it’s hard to take someone seriously when you’ve had a graphic description of them having to go to A&E more than once to have something removed when they hadn’t read the instructions properly.

So I sat with my pen and paper, and Ben’s old laptop, so that I could search for caterers. When Dad came home to check on me at teatime, he found me with a long list of crossed out options and the beginnings of a very mild but definite case of the panics.

‘I’ll cater for you if you like,’ he said, opening the cupboard doors and pulling out a few jars. One of my favourite programmes was called *Ready Steady Cook*. The chefs were presented with a random bag of ingredients, from which they had to produce a multi-dish meal in the space of twenty minutes. I loved it. I modelled my entire style of cooking on it, which is to say that I never planned ahead and usually just hoped that I would be able to produce something edible from whatever I had lying around. I ate a lot of pasta pesto. Dad, however, had the magic skills. A few minutes later he set a steaming plate in front of me, grated some cheese on top from great height, just for show, and watched as I dug in.

'You are a genius,' I said, talking with my mouth full but it was too tasty not to tell him straight away. Despite having eaten just before my nap, it was so good I cleared my plate. 'I don't doubt your skills at all. It's just that Mr King is quite a tricky customer. He comes to my shop every birthday and Christmas, and doesn't leave until he's looked through all of my stock, found it wanting and had me questioning my skills and wondering why on Earth he doesn't just go to Selfridges. Or Tiffany's. Goodness knows he can afford to.'

'He likes the personal touch,' Dad said. 'Anything he bought there would just be the same thing in a box that a dozen other husbands are buying. I bet none of those other husbands have ever taken their wives home the sort of luxurious and personal items you can source for him.'

'Last Christmas he went home with a dozen rude teddy bears,' I told my dad. 'One of them was wearing the sort of underwear that Lily sells. Another had a whip.' I didn't dare tell him about the one with the huge furry boner.

'Thank goodness you came up with the idea of a photoshoot with Cody for Christmas then. That did her a huge favour too. She's had quite a few bookings from his wife's friends off the back of it. Not to mention that the cheque he wrote her covered the rent for several months. No, if you need a caterer then look no further. He might scare you, but he can't scare me. I brought up twins on my own, though Ben only had the police and secret service arrive three times before he got his job.'

I kissed my dad's cheek and threw my arms around him. 'I don't think you have any idea what you're letting yourself in for, but I'm very grateful. Now, what do posh people eat at buffets? I don't think sausage rolls and cheese on sticks is going to cut it.'

'Leave it to me,' Dad said, guiding me out of the room. 'I've had a few ideas recently that I've been planning to try.'

I decided to trust him and took myself off to use his bathroom whilst I was upstairs anyway. A hefty dose of lavender bubble bath helped soothe the last of the tension from my shoulders, and by the time I got downstairs I found Eli fast asleep in my bed. I kissed his cheek and snuggled up against him. I didn't mean to wake him, but when he saw me and smiled, I was glad that I had.

'I only came in to sit down for a few minutes. One of the perils of not having a living room, I laid down on the bed instead and I've been snoring ever since,' he said, peeking under my dressing-gown to check what I was wearing underneath. It turned out not to be very much and his smile grew even wider. 'Not that I'm complaining, when I get to wake up to find you here too.' He began to demonstrate how happy he was to see me, and despite the stressful start to my day, I was relieved to note that it ended up being much more fun than I ever could have imagined.

I fully expected to sleep like a log, I usually did. Eli was very patient and very thorough. This time when the door knocking began at eight o'clock, even though I complained about being woken, at least I wasn't hungover. I let Mr King in, told Eli to brew a pot of coffee big enough for all of us, and fetched clean clothes before locking myself in the shower.

'This time it's the sodding photographer I'd booked. My business partner's wife so it was hard to refuse. Bloody well should have though. Broke her wrist skiing yesterday just before they were due to fly home,' he said, handing me a dainty cup, though I'd have preferred a bucket-sized serving of caffeine. 'If you can convince that lady friend of yours to do her magic, tell her I'll pay her twice what I did for the photoshoot.'

Chapter Twenty-Three

'Tell me this party is actually going to happen,' I said to Eli, as I checked my itinerary for the seventh time that morning.

He fiddled with his already perfect tie and ran a hand over his newly buzzed haircut. 'It's going to be fine. Your dad says he's got the food mostly prepared. There's plenty of time for him to do the finishing touches in the kitchen once you arrive. Lily is coming to help waitress, though there are only twenty-five people so I'm sure even if you end up having to serve lunch buffet style they will manage.' He kissed my cheek and headed to the front door.

Cody had been nervous at first about losing a day's preparation time ahead of her big exhibition, but the cheque that Mr King had given her had made the decision easier. It would allow her to close her gallery until the exhibition, and so actually she had more time free now than she had before and was thrilled. She had dressed for the role of chief photographer in a plain cotton muumuu. The fact that it was bright orange still made it more simple than many of her outfits and suited the effect that Mrs King had aimed for, of understated elegance. 'You look beautiful,' I told Cody, and she gave a twirl, her skirt flowing out to show turquoise and pink fabrics underneath. She took a green ribbon from her pocket and used it to tie up her hair.

'We are going to have a wonderful day,' she said, packing the last of her cameras into a bag and double checking that she had a stash of memory sticks and batteries.

Eli was outside, his car pulled up on the kerb as he loaded foil-covered trays that my dad handed him. Dad emerged, staggering under the weight of a large bowl. Eli took it from him and stowed it safely in the boot. The cover began to slip, and I saw what looked suspiciously like an over-sized orange, skewered with cheese and pineapple.

'Dad!' I exclaimed. 'I told you, these guys are posh, they're going to need some massively poncey food to be impressed. They probably don't eat anywhere that doesn't have a Michelin star.'

He laughed and gave my arm a quick squeeze. 'Don't panic. It's an orange scented bread, the skewers are grissini. The cheese is a variety of artisanal cheeses, none of which are stocked by supermarkets. They all took some sourcing, I can tell you. The pineapple is pineapple though, I couldn't quite work out how to fancy that up, but I'm pleased with it.'

So was I. In fact, I hadn't been able to eat any breakfast because of the nerves and so my mouth began watering at the thought. Dad handed me a paper wrapped parcel. 'There's a couple of slices from one of my test batches in here, with a bit of proper French butter. Don't get any crumbs on your nice dress.'

I didn't. It was so delicious that I ate every single morsel, licking my fingers to wipe crumbs from the paper. Screwing the wrapper up into a ball, I tucked it into my handbag and looked up to find Eli staring at me. 'If you looked at me that way you looked at that bread, I would die a happy man.'

'I'll look at you like that later if you help me survive today,' I promised him.

'I once took down a terrorist cell armed with nothing but a mobile phone and a ball of string. You're going to be fine today,' he assured me. 'And if all else fails, at least you know that the wine they serve is going to be decent.'

'I'm already planning on waking up tomorrow with a hangover more expensive than my flat.'

'That's my girl,' he said, kissing me and letting me climb into the car.

We arrived to find Mr King's country house a hive of activity. The florists were draping yards of tulle and lace around the banisters. Jars of fresh blooms in whites and yellows sat on every window-sill and shelf. Mrs King had dressed accordingly, in a knee-length, buttercup-coloured skirt-suit. Mr King had a slate-grey suit on, but even he had a yellow silk handkerchief and tie. He stood to attention as we entered, and I almost expected him to salute my dad when he walked in carrying a silver tray covered in intricately presented, mouth-watering amuse-bouche.

Dad was soon directed to the kitchen, and Cody to the study so that she could unpack her cameras and get set up. I was on duty to oversee and ensure that everything went to plan. Eli, having fulfilled his duty as our chauffeur and reassurer-in-chief, had brought his tablet and disappeared off to find somewhere quiet to work, or more likely to play online games with Ben who was waiting at home.

I buzzed around the garden ensuring that the gazebo was set up and decorated appropriately. A pedestal of tumbling blooms was placed at the front. Small speakers were hidden behind potted olive trees and bay plants. A couple of dozen chairs had been assembled in rows, facing the front, and draped in white cloth, tied with yellow satin bows. Mr King and I had argued about balloons. He felt that they weren't as classy as the look he wanted to achieve, but I had insisted that they were an integral part of a celebration. The silvery helium orbs that floated around the outskirts of the tent, tethered by curly strings the same colour as the sunflowers, lent a party vibe to the otherwise quiet surroundings.

The string quartet arrived and began to set up. That was one area where I hadn't had any input. When it came to classical music, I was totally out of my depth. Mr King had given me a list of excerpts that he wanted, and I'd passed it on. Whether his son and daughter-in-law had had any input was not discussed.

Checking my watch prompted me that we had half an hour to go before the guests were due to arrive. I went to touch base with Dad in the kitchen. He had silver trays of canapes ready to serve, and Lily was there chatting with him over a coffee as he slid a tray of fresh rolls into the oven. Thankfully knowing Lily for so long had led me to expect her turning up to serve food dressed in a French maid's costume so that didn't come as a shock. In fact, this one was more demure than others she sold, and whilst much of her cleavage was on display, you couldn't actually see down to her belly button, so I handed her a black apron to wear over the top and didn't insist on her changing into the spare dress that I'd packed just in case.

'It looks as though you have everything in hand. Why don't you stop and have some food before the guests come? You'll be busy enough after that checking that they're okay,' Dad suggested, handing me a glass of water and a plate of bread and cheese cubes.

By the time the first of the guests arrived, I was feeling fairly serene. Mr King greeted them at the door, and I had Lily stand behind him with a tray of canapes whilst I offered them a glass of champagne. I felt calm. I felt under control. And then my mobile rang.

I'd set it to vibrate, and so thankfully the noise was subtle. I ducked into the hall and went in search of a quiet room to take the call in, eventually ending up in the study. It had beautiful mahogany bookshelves lining every wall, and a deep red rug in the centre of the room. The double set of French doors at the back opened into the back garden, which was by now beginning to buzz with party-goers. Eli was hunched over his screen. He was either working away feverishly, or he was deeply ensconced in a game.

'Hi, Daisy speaking. Sorry it took me a moment to answer. Busy day.'

'It's about to get busier I'm afraid,' said a voice that I couldn't place. 'This is Kara, the celebrant. I'm afraid I've had a bit of an accident. Someone drove into the back of me.'

'Do you want me to send someone to pick you up?' I offered, wondering whether I could ask yet another favour and send Eli to collect her.

'That's very kind, but I'm currently sat in A&E waiting to have my leg set in plaster. I'm not going to be able to make it today.'

Chapter Twenty-Four

'No,' Eli said, shaking his head. He didn't take his eyes from the screen.

'I haven't said a word.'

'You didn't need to. I heard the call and whatever you need, I'm not doing it. I'm busy.'

'You're playing an online war game with Ben. You get enough of that at work.'

'Still not doing it. It's been crazy busy at work, I just want an hour off to shoot bad guys.'

'That's pretty much what you do at work too, isn't it?' But he was too busy tapping buttons to reply. I swore and sat in the leather chair at the drop leaf antique desk. It was hard to stay tense when you were sat in a comfy chair, and especially one that spun around. It didn't even squeak, unlike the stools at my counter at home. And then Mr King walked past the window. I span the chair so that he couldn't see me. 'What am I going to do?' I wailed.

Eli finally put the tablet down and looked up at me. 'This isn't a religious service, right?'

'Right.'

'So, you don't need an ordained minister. Why don't you just print a speech off the internet, thank them for coming, introduce the baby, and get them drunk on expensive wine?'

'Because I'm being paid to organise a naming ceremony, and not having someone here to run the ceremony is a pretty big gap. Mr King knows me. If I try and stand up there, he'll glare daggers and I'll melt into a pile of goop on the gazebo floor.' I thought about how much work had gone into organising the day, and how it would all be pointless thanks to a careless driver. I was going to have to refund

Mr King his deposit, not to mention pay for the wine and food that had been purchased. He'd never come to my shop again, which wasn't a bad thing, but neither would any of his colleagues and I'd been counting on picking up a few new commissions to get me through the long hot summer. Business picked up again once the weather got colder and people began to think about Christmas, but it was a long time to go until then. I had phone bills and new shoes to pay for. I began to cry.

Eli switched his tablet off, walked over and hunched in front of me. 'You know I can't bear to see you cry. Okay, I'm in, I'm going to celebrant like no-one has ever celebranted before.' I wasn't sure that made much sense, but he was saving my bacon, again, so I didn't argue with him. Thank goodness he had such innate style that he always looked good. All he needed was a speech, which we soon downloaded and personalised. I left him learning it, and we were back on track. In the kitchen Dad was humming as he worked. He dressed salads, handed Lily more platters to carry around and slid a tray of mini quiches into the oven. He was a blur of activity, and he had never looked happier.

In the garden, Cody was poised with her camera, taking snap after snap of people laughing, chatting and eating Dad's delicious snacks. It was amazing to see her Amazon-esque figure, so brightly coloured and eye-catching, become almost invisible as she melted into the background, capturing the day forever without becoming an intrusive part of it.

'The guest of honour has arrived,' Mr King announced, leading his son and daughter-in-law into the garden. In her arms she held a sleeping child. Quickly the guests crowded around to coo over the baby, who woke up to find a dozen fingers pointing at her, and promptly began to wail. 'More champagne,' Mr King proclaimed, leaving the mum to calm and soothe her baby.

I hurried off to find more alcohol. Instead I found Lily showing off her outfit to a gaggle of admiring women, and a couple of men. 'Lily,' I hissed, gesturing to her to put the apron back on again.

'I might have got a bit carried away,' she admitted, tucking her barely restrained cleavage away behind the black fabric. Instantly the young men who had been watching her discovered that they were needed elsewhere and vanished. Lily introduced me to her new friends.

'It's my fault,' squeaked a lady who had been almost hidden behind a ficus tree. I thought her name was Martha, but she'd ducked out of sight behind her friend so I couldn't tell for sure. Even her voice barely carried as far as where I was stood. 'My husband has had a fancy for something like that for years. I was just saying that I wished I was a couple of decades younger. I should have dressed up for him while I had the chance.'

'I don't dress for anyone else,' Lily told her. 'I wear outfits that I feel confident in. And as for being too old? What are you, fifty? I have people much older than you come in to my shop. I once sold an outfit like this to an eighty-year-old.'

The lady squeaked again and drew her cardigan around herself, despite the warmth of the day. 'Did she like it?'

'He was thrilled,' Lily confirmed. 'Apparently he had always wanted one but was too shy to go and buy it. Finally he just decided that if he didn't get it then, he was never going to. That's what I'm all about. If you need something to help you feel like the person you are inside, I'll help you find it. No judgement, only encouragement and understanding.'

'I still say less is more,' said a voice behind me which could have cut glass, it was so refined. 'Give me a silk nightie and a beautiful dressing-gown any day of the week. Sometimes it's not what you put on display, it's what they know you have wrapped up just for them.'

'You'd love Daisy's shop,' Lily told them.

'I do carry a wide range of elegant nightwear,' I said. The lady with the Radio Four voice squeezed her way through and came to stand where she could see us. She had a string of pearls around her neck and a diamond brooch on her fuchsia blouse. 'I sourced them myself, they're cut on the bias so they hang beautifully.' She looked tempted.

'What other costumes do you sell?' asked the first lady. I looked at her again, realising that she wasn't sat down, as I'd first assumed, but was in fact well under five-foot in height. It wasn't often that I saw people even shorter than Lily, who the lady was currently staring at adoringly.

'What takes your fancy?'

'My husband used to love Princess Leia,' admitted another woman.

'In the gold bikini?' Lily asked.

'Or as a kick-ass General?' I added. 'Between us we could help you with either or both.'

'My daughter left a novel behind when she went to university,' said one woman, draining her wine and leaning in as if she were letting us in on a secret. She was flushed and it was hard to know if it was from the booze or the conversation. 'I've never read anything like it. I never thought I'd be having racy dreams about cowboys.'

'Very popular,' Lily reassured her. 'We stock leather chaps.' She then had to explain what those were, at which point the woman giggled behind her hand. It was a good job that Lily hadn't told her that the ones she sold weren't designed to be worn with anything underneath. Not to mention the range of whips she also stocked.

'I could source you a Stetson,' I chipped in, hoping that that wasn't going to raise anyone's blood pressure enough to cause a stroke.

'Did you hear that, Enid? A cowboy hat. You mustn't get mixed up and wear that to church by mistake.'

'I'm more interested in the silk, Vera.'

'I like the ones Lily was telling me about with all the tassels,' another lady chipped in.

'I don't know, I've always been an M&S multi-pack girl myself, Maude.'

'I carry a range of knickers, too,' I told them. 'Dainty ones, but also French knickers which look a bit more like shorts if you prefer something less skimpy.'

'We ought to come to your shops,' Enid said. 'We could make it a ladies' day out, stop for lunch and a cocktail on the way home.'

'Is it nearby, dear?' Vera asked Lily. 'Your shop?'

'Oh, I couldn't actually go in,' Ethel said.

Lily tried to assure her that there was nothing to be scared of, but Ethel was not to be persuaded. Lily looked to me for help, but I could hardly pretend that I still didn't get nervous of going in myself.

'How about if you come to my shop and Lily brings some items across for you to look at? She really does stock some very fun items. We could make it into a bit of a party.'

This suggestion was greeted by a small cheer, and I handed my card to Vera who appeared willing to take charge and organise her friends.

Mr King had claimed that he was only expecting a couple of dozen guests today and a good many of them were busy with myself and Lily and not paying much attention to the baby. 'Perhaps we ought to re-join the main crowds,' I suggested, wondering what Mr King would say if he could hear the conversations we were having with his friends.

'Ladies and Gentlemen.' Eli's voice sounded clear into the garden. 'Please come and join me in the gazebo.' I could only hope that the ceremony script that we had found online would be perfect, as Eli welcomed the parents to the front of the tent. He glanced once more at his tablet to check his speech and began in a deep voice.

'We are gathered here today to celebrate the arrival of Serephina Allegra King-Smythe.' Eli launched into the talk. He thanked everyone for attending, and remarked on the role that they would play in Serephina's future. 'It has often been remarked that it takes a village to raise a child ...'

I sat at the back of the gazebo and admired him as he spoke. He looked elegant in his suit, confident and easily held the attention of the room. He talked about the role that Serephina's parents would play in bringing her up and how everyone could help them by modelling the kindness and generosity of spirit that they hoped she would meet throughout her life.

I hadn't been far from tears all day, and now I found myself welling up again, even though I knew that every word Eli was saying had just been cut and pasted together in a hurry when the original celebrant had cancelled. Delivered in Eli's rich timbre, it carried depth nonetheless.

Eli's eyes swept the crowd as he asked them to think about how they might welcome Serephina into their hearts and show her how much she was loved. His gaze caught mine, and for a moment I couldn't look away. He spoke again. 'I can already tell you that this is a blessed baby.' That wasn't on his script. As we were having a non-religious service, I hadn't expected any mention of blessings.

'She has more people here, celebrating her arrival and wishing her well, than many other children. Standing here before you I know that she is going to have a lifetime of knowing that she is wanted and loved. She will never feel alone, and whilst I'm sure that you have all brought her generous gifts, the love that you have shown by coming here today is the greatest gift that any human being can give another.'

He continued, no longer reading from his papers. 'Isn't that what children are about after all? Two people coming together and deciding that they love each other so much, that they want to increase that, create new joy, and so they have a child.' It felt like an intimate conversation, despite the number of people in between us. Eli couldn't be asking me to have a baby with him though, could he? We'd barely found space for his pants and socks in my bedroom. Where would we fit a baby?

Chapter Twenty-Five

No-one mentioned what they had thought of Eli's speech on the way home. Dad had been stuck in the kitchen and hadn't heard it. I presumed that either Lily hadn't either, or hadn't heard the same subtext in it that I had. Back at home, Cody retreated to her own place to sort through the photos. She wasn't planning to print them until after her exhibition, but she wanted to make sure she had them safely backed up and planned to email a few advance images to the family to tide them over in the meantime.

Dad had a mountain of washing up to do, but he announced that he was going to have a nap before he started on it. Lily looked like she was going to hang around until I said that, given how much he had helped me out by providing the catering, I was going to clean up whilst he slept. After that, Lily suddenly decided that she might be needed at work after all.

'Isn't she going to change first?' Eli asked, watching her walk away in her maid's outfit, now without the apron over the top.

'She'll make more sales if she goes in that. I just hope they have a few more in stock.'

Eli grinned. 'Tea or more champagne?' he offered, holding up a silver gift bag. Mrs King had thanked us all for our help and handed us each a wrapped bottle as we left. Although she was still not completely happy at the idea of a secular ceremony, she was at least pleased that she had been able to celebrate the birth of her grandchild. Given that it wasn't a decision that made for an easy compromise, I was glad that she had taken it so well and accepted the conciliatory gesture for what it was. For her son's part, he had looked thrilled at seeing so many of their family and friends and being able to introduce them to the baby. He had stood up to thank everyone for coming and surprised his wife with a sapphire ring as a thank you for everything she'd been through to bring their daughter into the world. As we'd left I'd seen the three of them, baby in the middle, sharing a cuddle and remarking quietly on how lucky they were to have each other.

Eli had seen it too and had rested a gentle hand in the small of my back as we both fell silent, probably thinking about how our experiences of our own parents had been so different. Now, stood in the quiet of Dad's kitchen, washing trays and passing them to Eli to dry, I wondered if he was going to say any more about his speech. 'Tea,' I told him when he hadn't said anything for a few minutes. 'If I drink any more alcohol now I'll fall asleep.'

He laughed, deep in his chest. 'You've earned it. You took what could have been a tricky family dynamic and gave them a party that made them all happy.'

'Only because you stepped in at the last minute.'

'Anything to help.'

He distracted me from asking about his speech by kissing me. 'I need a bath,' I pointed out.

'Want someone to wash your back?'

I did. My front too, but Dad was asleep upstairs and it felt wrong to risk him overhearing us.

'How about you go down and chill the champagne? I'll join you downstairs afterwards.'

Between the bath, the champagne and the orgasms I slept long and deeply. Grateful that I hadn't booked any appointments for the day after the naming ceremony, I woke up in Eli's arms and stayed there, enjoying the soft rise and fall of his chest underneath me as he slept. His phone vibrated softly on top of the trunk that we used as a bedside table. He didn't stir. It stopped ringing and a moment later my phone buzzed too. I shifted, trying not to wake him, as I picked it up and checked the display. Dad was upstairs so, as long as it wasn't Ben, I had no intention of answering. Number withheld. I dropped it and closed my eyes again.

Eli's phone began to hop as it buzzed, but this time it was accompanied by a loud ringing. 'Ben.' He cursed. 'How many times do I have to tell him not to change the settings on my phone. I set it to silent for a reason. He must have given himself permission to make it ring anyway when he calls.'

He sat up, the sheet falling to his waist, as he reached across to pick his phone up. 'I'm busy, and for once I don't care that you know it's because I'm in bed with your sister. Call me back later.'

'I don't have a sister, but I suggest that you get your backside out of bed and get dressed. I'll be with you in ten minutes,' I heard clearly over the line.

'Yes, Boss,' Eli said, instantly waking up more fully, ending the call and reaching for his pants. 'Sounds like she's back from the spa and ready to get us working hard again.'

'I heard. Her voice really does carry, doesn't it?' I said.

Eli took a quick shower while I made him a coffee. He was dressed one minute before the knocking began. Eli took the Boss upstairs to Dad's kitchen while I showered. Given that something urgent must have come up at work, I washed my hair, shaved my legs and spent ages choosing my outfit to give them time to talk. I had narrowed it down to my black leggings and a floaty pink tunic, or a blue sundress with little daisies around the bottom when the door at the bottom of the stairs opened, and I turned to find Eli there drumming his fingers against the wall.

'The Boss asks if you can join us.' He didn't look happy, but I didn't have time to wonder what was going on as he turned and walked back upstairs. I threw the leggings and top on and followed him up.

'As I was saying,' Boss lady continued, 'the captain has been spotted in London. He was walking near our office and we don't know why.'

'Couldn't someone go and ask him?' Everyone turned to stare at me as I spoke. I shrugged. 'You asked me up here. Don't blame me if I'm not up to date.' The Boss nodded once and then gave a brief but concise update on the situation. Not one unnecessary word was used. 'I still don't get why no-one else in your office knows that Jean-Luc is over here,' I said when she finished.

'Because with the lack of evidence of what's going on, we've decided that it's best not to publicise his sudden and unusual appearance. Unfortunately, that means we're operating under the radar, within the context of a room full of people trained to be vigilant. As you can imagine, it has been a challenge.'

I looked at Ben. He was hunched over his laptop. Erin glanced at him, concern evident in her loving gaze. 'I've been tracking all of his bank accounts,' he said. 'Nothing. And that's unusual in itself. He has access to a large number of accounts that would be available if he needed to go under the radar for work. He even has a couple of personal accounts. I'm not sure if his colleagues even know about those. They took me a few minutes to find so they're pretty secure. He must be using cash.'

Ben wasn't being boastful. If he said that the accounts were tricky to find then they were.

'Have you tried calling hotels?' All the eyes in the room were on me and I quickly flushed red and waited for them to point out that they were experts and had of course already considered this approach.

'Do you remember how hard it was to find Ben when there were only half a dozen hotels?' Eli replied. Then it was Erin's turn to blush.

'If he's paying for things without us being able to trace him then he's definitely staying somewhere without registering in any of his known aliases.' The Boss lady spoke slowly as if I were a child. 'Which brings us all up to date. I want strategies, people. Plans. How are we going to find the Captain?'

No-one had yet explained why the Boss had requested that I join them. I assumed Eli had made his objections on the grounds of my personal safety already and had either been overruled or reassured. I wondered how long it would be before anyone explained the reasons to me.

Eli pulled out his mobile and tapped at the screen, as if all of the answers were waiting in cyberspace. Perhaps if he Googled 'how to find a missing spy' we'd be onto something. Ben stared at his own screen. Only Erin moved around, making tea and setting a plate of dad's oat biscuits on the table. It was busy work, letting her feel like she was doing something but without coming up with any answers.

She handed me a mug and I took a seat next to Eli. No-one looked at me. Finally, I coughed. The Boss glanced up. 'Is there anything I can do to be useful? I assume I'm not here because you like my taste in frilly knickers?'

I expected Eli to make a joke about getting inside my knickers, or perhaps because of the present company to just give me a sly wink to let me know that he was thinking of it, but I got no response at all. If anything, he concentrated more closely on whatever he could see on his phone. Whatever had led to me being included, it wasn't by Eli's request.

'None of our traditional approaches to finding people have worked. You seem to have something of a reputation for tracking down those who don't want to be found.' I wondered whether the Boss was angry that we had interrupted her spa break but she gave no more sign than that. 'Sometimes it is useful to think a little more creatively. We didn't all agree on that.' She shot a glare at Eli. 'But I decided that we needed a new way of looking at this. Eli, show her the video.'

He muttered to himself as he reached for Ben's laptop and clicked a few buttons. 'It's as though he wants us to know he's here; he's been filmed on our CCTV walking not too far from our office, but as soon as we get downstairs he's gone, and as we said, there's no sign of him staying anywhere. It's strange. If he wants to stay under the radar, why pop up where he knows we'll see him?'

'Is he trying to give you a message?' I asked. Suddenly all the eyes in the room were on me. I hesitated, but no-one else spoke so I carried on, talking before I'd really thought through what I meant. 'Perhaps he knows that his disappearance from his office in Paris is being kept quiet, or at least suspects it, so he doesn't want anyone to know for sure that he's here. But he needs help, so he's hoping that you'll pick up on it and find a way to get in touch.' The Boss nodded, and I felt a bit braver about carrying on. 'Does he know who is likely to see the surveillance tapes?'

'I showed him the set up when he was last over,' my brother explained. 'I think you're right, Daisy. Look at this bit of the film. He doesn't come into the building where he would be picked up by the main security guards. He just passes the corner which is covered by the additional cameras set up to protect our office which are sent directly to me.'

'So, he's trying to reach you deliberately? Is there any pattern to what time you're picking him up on his walks?'

Ben took the laptop back and typed a few lines. He shook his head. 'He's out there first thing in the morning some days, late in the evening on others. There's no set amount of time in between his visits, and no set amount of time that he stays, though it's never more than about three minutes.'

'Maybe you need to be out there waiting for him,' I suggested.

'I've gone undercover in a lot of places,' Eli began. 'Waiting outside a building full of spooks and hoping not to get spotted is asking for trouble.'

'Shame you're not invisible,' I mused. No-one found it funny or helpful.

Chapter Twenty-Six

The Boss headed off shortly after that, telling us to get in touch once we had a plan. She seemed more confident than anyone else felt that this would happen. For my part, I felt out of my depth. I knew that Eli would want me kept at a safe distance from whatever was happening.

'Anyone for dinner?' I offered.

'I'm a bit bored of beans on toast,' Ben said.

I wanted to tell him not to be rude and point out that my cookery skills were not really that basic, but it had been a long day and frankly, he was correct. I couldn't really face turning on the oven and risk heating the room up any more. 'Fish and chips?'

'We grabbed burgers for our working lunch,' Eli said.

I was out of ideas. Luckily, as I looked out of the window in search of inspiration, as well as the beginning of a beautiful pink sunset, I saw Dad and Cody return. Cody had a camera strung around her neck. She'd probably been finishing up her shoot for the exhibition. I clicked my fingers. 'Got it.'

'Pizza?' Ben asked hopefully.

'No, but I can ring for some.'

'I'll order it online, then we don't need to use the phone.' My brother didn't make calls if he could help it, preferring to use online ordering forms wherever possible. He claimed that this reduced the areas where mistakes could be made, as no-one could dispute the order if it was written down in black and white, but I knew that it was because he didn't like talking to people he didn't know if he could help it.

'Do you remember seeing Cody at the party last week?' I asked Eli.

He shook his head. 'I was in the study working for most of the time that we were there, though.'

'Only for the first hour while we set up,' I pointed out. 'After that you were with me for most of it, running the ceremony, and afterwards for the food.'

'What are you getting at?' Eli asked. His tone wasn't as grumpy as his words might suggest. He was used to my thought processes and wanted to know whether I'd stumbled onto something. If I had, it might be purely that: a lucky stumble. Despite the Boss's feeling that I was good at finding people, so far it had been more luck than judgement that had contributed. Not to mention a dogged determination not to give up, and with no personal connection, I couldn't claim to feel the same for Jean-Luc. It had been my fear of losing Ben and upsetting my dad that had powered us to drive hundreds of miles last time. It had made me search every hotel, pub and cafe in North Wales, and get on a ferry in the middle of the night in the middle of a storm. It had brought Ben back safely. Could I help do the same again now for the Captain?

'How would you describe Cody?' I asked. Eli was still none the wiser for why I was asking but I could tell that I'd caught his interest. 'Be polite,' I cautioned him. And Ben, for whom that was never a given. My brother's lack of tact could lead to his honesty being brutal.

'Tall,' Eli began.

'Colourful,' Erin contributed.

'Kind,' Ben said, and I wanted to throw my arms around him and hug him. This wasn't the kind of thing he usually noticed. 'And loud.' That was the kind of thing that affected Ben more. He was pretty sensitive to people who impacted on his personal space. Me, I found Cody warm and friendly, but I could see how Ben having a new woman around who was interested in him and his life might take him a bit of getting used to.

I turned to Eli. 'When we were at the naming ceremony the other day, how would you have described Cody then?'

'I told you, I didn't see her.' He shrugged.

I gestured to Ben to pass me his laptop. Loading up my own email I turned the screen so that Eli could see it too. 'Cody sent me these this morning. She thought I might like her to print a few later.' I scrolled through. There were shots of Eli standing up to welcome the baby. More of him giving his speech and a couple of me welling up at the back. These pictures weren't for Mr King and his family; they were just bonus shots that she had captured as she had tried to record highlights of the entire day. There were a few of Eli eating some of Dad's amazing canapes, and one of the two of us relaxing afterwards with a well-earned glass of champagne. You could see the relief on our faces that the day had gone well. We were sat in deckchairs on the beautifully manicured lawn, holding hands loosely. I had my eyes closed and was capturing the last few rays of the evening sun. Eli was watching me and had the smallest hint of a smile. I didn't usually like having too many photos of myself, but I was desperate to get this one printed and framed. It was one of the most beautiful pictures of us together I'd ever seen.

'I don't remember her taking this,' Eli said, leaning in to get a better look. 'You look pretty.'

I flushed a little. Even though Eli and I had been together for six months and were just about living together now, it had taken us ten years to get to this stage and sometimes I still couldn't quite believe that we were together. I loved it when he made a sweet comment. Perhaps that was what was behind his gaze in the photo too. Sometimes it was the little reminders of how far we'd come that gave me pause.

'Nice as the photo is, how exactly does this help us right now?' Eli's voice snapped me back to the present, and his impatience reminded me of the pressure that he was under, so I didn't take it personally.

'You're not quick enough when you wait until you spot him to leave the office and go out in search of him. Besides, if you suddenly go running out at full speed it's hardly going to be a subtle exit.' They nodded as I spoke. 'You need to be outside waiting, but there's a reason why he's not approaching you directly so you need to be in the background, unnoticed, so that you can suss out what's going on. If you and Taylor took it in turns to do stakeouts, you could dress as photographers.'

'Or homeless people,' Erin chipped in. 'There's a *Big Issue* seller near where I go for lunch. I could cry when I see people walk past her as if she isn't there. I buy a copy from her every week and she's lovely.'

'So where is Taylor?' I asked. 'Maybe we ought to see what he thinks?'

Eli threw his head back and laughed. It was a stark contrast to the tension he had shown only moments earlier. 'Our French colleagues contacted the office to ask whether his being stopped at the border was related to any investigations. The Boss called him and screamed at him. By all accounts he asked if he could go to a war zone somewhere this week just to get out of the way until she calms down.'

Chapter Twenty-Seven

Eli twirled the spaghetti on his fork until the twines were covered, but then he kept turning it around and around as he thought. Finally, when I worried that he was in danger of wrapping his entire meal into a giant ball I interrupted his daydreaming.

'What did Boss lady say?'

'She liked your idea,' he said, using his knife to scrape the excess pasta off so that he could take a normal sized bite. I waited as he chewed. 'She said, and I quote, "If only the rest of you had as much sense as that girl".' I nearly high-fived him for that, but though normally he would have been so proud of me for that kind of praise, today he still looked distracted. I found out why with his next sentence. 'She wants you out there too.'

'I presume that you told her no?'

'It didn't go down well. She's not used to being refused.'

'She isn't my boss though, so she can't really order me, can she?' I thought about how worried Eli had been when he'd seen that I was in Paris. As exciting as the idea of helping him at work was, I didn't want to be the cause of any more stress for him.

'She says that I stand too much chance of missing him if I'm out there alone. She doesn't want to let anyone else know that he's here, and so it's either you or Ben out there too.' I pictured Ben outside, pretending to be homeless or with just a camera to hide behind. He'd be lost without his phone or his laptop and if anyone were rude or aggressive towards him, he'd be helpless. If he was out there then I'd want to be there too, looking after him.

'I'm not sure Ben would be much help outside,' I admitted.

Eli's shoulders slumped with exhaustion. 'I didn't think so

either. Besides, the Boss wants him tracking the Captain online to see if anything shows up. So, it looks like it's you and me.'

I leaned across the table and kissed his cheek. I wanted to tell him that we'd have fun working together, but of course that wasn't the point. It was precisely the reason why I'd been so concerned when Lily had asked me to go to Paris. If Jean-Luc had been compromised, then his life was in danger.

'I'll be careful. I promise.'

'We're not going to engage with him, just see if we can find out what he's playing at, and it'll be in public so hopefully it won't be any more dangerous than your spa trip.' I wasn't sure if Eli was trying to reassure me or himself. I reached for his hand. He drew me in for a hug, stroked my hair and kissed me, softly and gently on the lips.

After Eli had washed up and I'd been for a bath upstairs in Dad's flat, we headed for my room and loaded a film on my laptop. We snuggled up in bed to watch it. Usually this would lead to a spot of making out, and often we'd get so distracted that we'd end up missing most of the film and would have to start it again after we'd finished making love, unless we were so tired that we fell asleep. There were a lot of films where I'd only ever watched the first ten minutes.

Tonight though, Eli was staring resolutely at the screen. Half way through I paused the film and turned to look at him. 'Are you ready to talk yet?'

He shook his head and moved to restart the film. I moved the laptop out of his reach so that he couldn't. 'I was watching that,' he protested.

'You weren't.'

'How do you know?'

'Because it has been half an hour, and nothing has been blown up and no-one has taken their clothes off. If you had been watching it then you would have been complaining by now.' He didn't reply to that. 'Not to mention that the heroine just got proposed to with a ring in her dessert.'

'That's just unhygienic,' he complained. 'Not to mention clichéd.'

'Exactly. Which is how I know that you're not paying any attention.' He grunted. I chose to hear it as confirmation that I was correct. 'I'll try my best to stay out of trouble.'

Finally, he snapped out of the funk he'd been in and drew me against him for a hug. 'I know you will. And honestly, I'd probably be even more worried if I were out there with Ben. I wouldn't be able to take my eyes off him, not that I can from you, but that's in an entirely different way.'

'Would you rather I called the Boss and said no?'

Eli sighed. 'No, I don't want to be that kind of man. I don't want to stop you, even if it's because I care about you so much. That way leads to controlling behaviour, telling you that you can't do something because of how it makes me feel. I can't do that to you again. It's manipulative. I know I came pretty close in Paris, and I nearly broke up yours and Lily's friendship. I'm realising that with me and Ben, Erin and Taylor in this world and around you all the time, I can't pretend that I can keep you separate from it forever. So, I choose to open my life up. Even though it scares the shit out of me to do so.'

Finally, having let go of the tension and talked about what was bothering him, we snuggled and moments later Eli fell asleep in my arms. He didn't have any nightmares that night either.

In the morning I woke Eli up with a coffee and a kiss. He took a long deep swallow of his drink and I took the opportunity to talk whilst he was still either too sleepy or too busy to argue. 'It's going to be okay. I'm happy to be out there with you. Happier about it than you are at any rate, but I understand why you're reluctant. I've decided that I want to grow old and grey with you, so I'm going to be careful. We both are. We're going to find Jean-Luc, safely, and then we're going to carry on with our lives, together.'

Eli didn't look completely convinced by my speech, but he was too much of a professional to allow his nerves to stop him.

'You remember what he looks like?' Eli asked me, again.

'Ben showed me every photo your office has of him and then a few more from his personal cloud yesterday. If we ever find him, I'm going to tell him to change his password and make his account a lot more secure if he's going to take photos like that. They were ...' I fanned myself with my hand.

'Won't make any difference. Ben could still access them,' Eli assured me. 'But maybe we should introduce him to Lily once this is all over.' He handed me back his empty mug and headed for the shower. I made to follow him in, but he stopped me.

'Tempted as I am, we need to stay sharp today. And that means not turning up for work already feeling in need of more sleep. If you give me five minutes now, I'll pack our bags while you take a turn after.'

Nothing I could do could persuade him, not even unveiling a new selection of underwear that Lily had given me and which I'd sworn to her that I'd never wear. Eli had growled when he'd seen it and turned the shower dial to cold, but he hadn't climbed out. I'd considered keeping the outfit on under my clothes, but the knickers, or what passed for them, left an awful lot of me at risk for catching a draught and so I changed them for more substantial items. Eli didn't look any happier at that either, but I pointed out that he'd be able to concentrate more easily if he wasn't distracted by what I was or wasn't wearing. He shook his head as he let himself out of my flat and up to my dad's so that he could make us a packed lunch.

Ben had brought some cameras home with him from the office and he demonstrated them as we got ready to leave. 'Don't you just point and click?' I asked him.

'If these were regular cameras then yes,' he agreed. 'These, however, are modified to include a few elements that I designed. They have built-in microphones that can be activated with this dial which resembles the settings toggle. Also, they have a higher resolution than you can buy on the open market currently.'

'Would they let us read a car registration from space?' I asked.

'Not quite,' Ben answered, ignoring my joke, 'but not far off. Also, you can be stood half a mile away and this microphone could detect if you farted.'

'Good job we didn't have beans on toast for tea,' I muttered.

Chapter Twenty-Eight

Eli suggested that we wait at either end of the road outside the office. It was a busy stretch, full of tourists, harassed commuters and even more harassed and exhausted new parents pushing buggies. The building that Eli and Ben worked in was a fairly nondescript office block from the outside. It was a deliberate attempt to keep attention away from the highly secretive work going on inside. They were a small team hidden in amongst many others who carried out far more routine government business. All the better to be hidden in plain sight, they hoped.

Eli had taken me in, once, back when we had been searching for Ben. I'd been distracted by the regular office feel of it. It was only afterwards that I'd come to understand the inbuilt security, the biometrics in the door handles ensuring that only permitted staff could open them, and the voice recognition in the lift which would lock between floors if it picked up an unexpected occupant.

Today, Eli was staking out the view from the safety of a coffee shop, camera round his neck, pretending to scan through pictures he had supposedly taken already on a fake holiday. I envied him the access to caffeine and toilets, but I had the advantage of an easier setting for my cover identity. I was in the park and it felt entirely natural to have a camera there. I tried to remember some of Cody's tips and took a few shots of the hydrangeas as I used them to offer me some shelter from view of passers-by whilst allowing me a direct line of sight, through the gaps in the blooms, to the main road.

Nothing. I fiddled with the settings on the camera, trying to zoom in so that I could get a close-up which wasn't blurry. It didn't work. My next few shots were just as out of focus. I tried pressing the button that had a picture of a flower on it. Still no luck. My mobile rang.

'Hi Eli, is it okay to talk while we're on a stake-out?'

Eli's laugh rumbled down the phone line to me. 'Every other person in this café is playing on their phones. I looked out of place until I picked mine up. Ben texted me, he said you turned on your location tracker. Have you spotted anything?'

'There are some gorgeous blooms. Do you think I should branch out and start selling flowers too?'

'I meant, have you spotted Jean-Luc?' His voice was still low, but the humour had gone, so I tried my best to get serious too.

'No, no sign. I must have set off one of Ben's modifications by mistake. I'll try not to press anything else.'

We hung up, and chastened by the call, I gave up on taking photographs. One of the benches was in the shade of a horse chestnut tree but another was catching some beautiful rays. I headed for it and secured my space just before a young couple reached it. The girl shot me a dirty look, but thirty seconds later they were safely ensconced on the shaded seat and buried tonsil deep in each other, so I didn't feel too guilty. I took some factor-fifty sun cream from my bag and began to rub it on to my arms. I reached my shoulders, making sure that they were covered underneath the thin straps of my dress.

My phone rang again. 'Want me to come and help you?'

'How on earth can you see me from where you are?' I asked Eli.

'Ben looped the CCTV from the park to my mobile. You see the camera on the roof of the pagoda opposite you?' I looked, finally spotting it hidden underneath a couple of pigeons. I gave it a tiny finger wave. 'I'd forgotten how boring stake-outs were,' Eli complained.

'You'd rather we were going in somewhere, all guns blazing?'

'If it were just me, maybe, but given that the Boss has put you in the mix too, I'm relieved that it's this quiet. In fact, I'm going to use the facilities whilst there's nothing happening. I've had to drink three cups of tea to hold my space. I never realised how precious a spot at this coffee shop was. I swear, there are two mums with buggies outside trying to psych me out so they can nab my table.'

I laughed as I hung up, shifting again to ensure that I could see as much of the road as possible whilst Eli was occupied elsewhere. There was nothing to see though, but for buses and taxis muscling their way past pedestrians and the odd driver who had braved the central London traffic. I assumed that Eli had finished in the bathroom and had successfully held on to his seat. For my part, I wished that I had thought to pack a book, or even a magazine, though I knew I would have been too busy watching my surroundings to read it. Sighing with boredom, I rang Lily.

'Hi bestie, what's up?'

'Nothing,' I told her. 'About an hour of nothing already and plenty more to go it seems.'

'Want me to come and join you? I can get out of work for a bit. I'll just tell my manager that I've got women's problems. He doesn't know that my main problem is him. He's so scared that I'll try and talk to him about periods that he'll let me go, no trouble.'

'Better not,' I said quickly, 'though I'd love to hang out. I'm supposed to be paying attention and you know if you come over that we'll get distracted.'

'I'm great at stake-outs,' Lily demurred.

'You are. When we were looking for Cody I enjoyed watching with you, though the chances that we'd find her when we ended up in the pub were probably pretty low, and I'm not sure I was much use when we got back outside again, I was that tipsy.'

'We had fun though.'

'We did,' I assured her. And then, out of the corner of my eye, I spotted someone, a man, eyes fixed down on the path in front of him, ignoring the teenagers who were now practically humping through their clothes on the bench. He passed right in front of me, and there was no mistaking it. I waited until he was safely past, quickly said goodbye to Lily then hung up and called Eli. 'I've found the Captain.'

Chapter Twenty-Nine

'Don't lose him,' Eli advised.

'I figured that. How close should I get?'

'How many people are between you? Stay close enough not to lose sight of him, not so close that you scare him off.' *Helpful.* I'd have pointed out just how much his advice hadn't aided me, but he wouldn't appreciate my sarcasm. And also, he had already hung up.

If I were him, staking out a suspect from a coffee shop, I'd have paid as I ordered to make sure that I could leave at any time without having to wait for a bill or risk running off without paying. Assuming that Eli had done the same, he was probably no more than a minute or two behind me, especially given that he actually enjoyed staying fit and didn't only go to aerobics classes when his best friend dragged him to one. He'd probably be able to track the Captain all day without getting knackered. Or getting blisters.

The new sandals which I had mistakenly put on that morning, assuming that they would be suitable for standing around in because they were almost flat, were in fact rubbing against my little toe now that I had to actually move in them. I grumbled to myself as I lengthened my stride, trying to keep up without breaking into an actual jog.

Ahead of me, the Captain was moving apace, weaving between tourists as he re-joined the crowds on Tottenham Court Road. Luckily he was tall, as well as being lean, and even though I could seldom see his black leather jacket or jeans from a distance, the dishevelled mop of his salt-and-pepper hair rose clear above the heads of those around him. The smells from the fast food restaurants which lined the street near the station made my stomach rumble as I marched, complaining at being told to move with no additional fuel. No matter; there would be time to find something when this was over. Eli was bound to catch up with him soon and I'd be able to drop away.

The Captain paused, and I stopped in my tracks, desperately trying to remember to look like I had a legitimate reason to stop too. It would have been more convincing if the girl walking behind me hadn't unceremoniously crashed into my backside and nearly sent us both flying. I apologised to her and she apologised to me, despite that fact that I had clearly caused the accident. By the time I'd composed myself, I caught just a glimpse of Jean-Luc as he ducked down a side street.

I followed him, risking a quick turn of the head to see if I could spot Eli behind me. I couldn't, but that didn't mean that he wasn't there. He was a professional, after all. The crowds were more sparse, and I was worried that the Captain would spot me. I lifted the camera to my eye and pretended that I was taking photos. Honestly, it probably made me even more conspicuous. There was little to see save white vans, now grey with dirt, and pigeons. I clicked off a couple of shots, kidding myself that I was capturing the turquoise of the pigeons' wings catching the rays of sunshine which made it past the scaffolding and gleamed iridescently. Usually pigeons were the vermin of the sky. There were so many of them, they covered benches with their poo and made walking under bridges treacherous for the same reason. It had been a long time since I had found one beautiful. No wonder Cody was such an uplifting person to spend time with. She was used to finding beauty in everything.

I was snapped out of my daydreaming by the angry beeping of a car horn. Jean-Luc had crossed the road, barely making it to the other side ahead of a motorbike. The L-plate on the back of the bike fluttered as the driver turned to avoid hitting him. The driver shouted angrily but Jean-Luc ignored him and kept walking. The driver would have to get used to swerving to avoid witless pedestrians if he was ever going to keep riding in London. His temperament was already perfectly suited to doing so, it seemed.

I waited until the road cleared before I followed. It was a few seconds that I didn't want to lose, but rather that than get run over and have to explain to the Boss lady that I had both lost the Captain and landed myself in hospital for my troubles. Staying about fifty metres behind, I finally made it across as Jean-Luc turned the corner again.

I paused, giving up all pretence of my disguise and flattened my body against the wall of the building. Leaning past the corner, I risked a few quick glimpses to see where he was headed. He didn't seem to be looking behind him, so I took that as a sign that he hadn't spotted my clumsy attempts at a tail. The road took him past a handful of residential buildings, nondescript and plain and yet probably far more expensive than I could ever dream of affording. Mind you, the same would be true for my own flat if it weren't for it having been in the family for a couple of generations already.

The Captain was growing more careful now, turning his head constantly. He darted right, and I hustled to keep up. There was maybe ten metres between us now. I was close, too close, but he was walking fast, and I was almost jogging. My breathing grew ragged as I kept up. He crossed again. I followed. Hurrying, dodging cars.

He turned left, and though I'd grown up on these streets I'd got so turned around I couldn't place where we were. More corners. As soon as he turned one I ran to catch up so that I didn't lose him. Finally, he slowed again. I stopped, bent almost double, sucking in greedy lungfuls of oxygen. Had he spotted me? Was that why he had stopped?

There was a tree, a large Maple, and I tried to duck behind it. In the distance I could hear him arguing. I risked a quick peek. There was no-one near him. He had his back to me. I risked watching more. He held a mobile, which he barked into. I couldn't understand the language, but the intent was clear. The Captain was angry. His hand wove emphatically through the air as he shouted. Then he paused, listened once more and uttered a string of guttural words, most likely curses given the vehemence with which he spat them out.

He hung up, dumping the phone back into his jacket pocket. His shoulders dropped, and he rubbed his face with both hands, before resuming his aimless walking. I counted to ten and then followed on. This time he walked slowly. I could keep up, but my shoes rubbed and I winced with each step. I stopped to fiddle with them, hoping that if I loosened a strap I could limit the damage they were doing to my poor toes. When I looked up again, the Captain was gone.

Chapter Thirty

I rang Eli. 'I lost him,' I said, expecting Eli to be pissed off but hopefully not surprised. For a novice spy I thought I'd done pretty well to get this far without the Captain picking up that I was tailing him.

'He's in the newsagent. Take a second, relax, you're doing really well.'

'Do I follow him in?'

'No, wait where you are. You can pick him up when he comes out. I'll go in and see what he bought in case it tells us anything.'

'Please can you grab me a packet of plasters while you're in there?'

Eli grunted, which I hoped meant that he would, but before I could double check Jean-Luc came out of the shop. I picked up my camera, turned my back to him just for a second and pretended that I was taking photos of the reflections in a car window. Instead, I used them to keep track of which direction he was heading in so that, a moment later, I could follow on.

He walked slowly now, not glancing around him at all, so I risked closing the distance a little and left the camera hanging loosely at my neck. Eventually he found his way back towards Edgware Road and I recognised where I was again. We'd covered a distance of about two miles, but we'd doubled back so many times we'd probably walked at least half that far again.

As he turned back onto the main road, I gave up any pretence of holding back; there were crowds again and it would be easy to tuck myself behind a group of random people and pretend that I was with them if the Captain turned around. He didn't. I rang Eli as I walked.

'Did you get any clues from the shop?'

'Nothing I can make sense of. He bought postcards and a lottery ticket. Careful, he's crossing the road.'

I hung up, took a moment longer than Jean-Luc had to wait for the red double-decker to pass me, and then crossed myself. Too late. He was gone.

'I've lost him,' I told Eli. 'Really, this time. Where are you?'

'Hold tight, I'll be with you in a minute.' It was closer to thirty seconds, and Eli appeared behind me. I jumped.

'How did you do that?'

'Training. Lots of training, and practice. But you did well for a newbie.'

'Not really, he's gone.'

Eli handed me a box of plasters. 'Here, do what you need to do, and we'll start looking. He came back this way for a reason. We'll do a bit of recon just in case, then head back and talk to the Boss. See if she can make any sense of all of this.' Eli winced when I took my sandal off and he saw the blood all over my toes. 'When they train us to deal with torture, they usually assume that someone else will be hurting us, not that we'll be injuring ourselves.'

'They train you to be tortured?'

Eli shrugged as if it were no big deal, but it was huge to me. I filed his reaction away to unpick later. He was getting restless. I cleaned my foot as much as I could with the tissue he handed me, covered my toe with several plasters and tried to ease my sandal back on. It stung, but no longer felt like sandpaper on an open wound. 'Can you walk?' he asked. I nodded. 'Let's go.'

We took opposite sides of the street, keeping each other in view as we walked. I watched Eli above the roofs of the cars between us. He kept facing forward, but his gaze swept over everything he passed. I tried to do the same. The roads got wider and busier, and as we reached Marylebone Road Eli crossed back to be with me.

'Sorry,' I told him. 'I messed up. I swear, I didn't take my eyes off him for more than a second.'

Eli sighed, but then put his arm around me and shook his head. 'Don't worry. It happens to all of us. I once lost a guy I'd followed for five miles. Ended up in the back streets of Moscow, lost, no back-up, and if I'd been found there I'd have been disappeared. No-one would ever have found me.'

'Really? You really want to scare me like this? I'm never going to want you to travel again.'

'I got home okay in the end. But you can understand why I wanted to keep you as far from the world I'm in as I could now?'

I nodded. 'Come on, I'll show you how Lily and I do stake-outs. I'm taking you to the pub.'

'There's one near here. In fact,' he glanced around him, 'yes, Daisy, you're a genius.' He planted a smacker of a kiss on my cheek.

'Ben's the genius in my family, but if you kiss him like that I might get jealous.'

Eli laughed. 'I took the Captain for a drink here once. A couple of years ago. He was staying in a hotel nearby, we'd had a big meeting about a new group we wanted to monitor together. Maybe he's trying to give us a message? But why wouldn't he let us know? Something strange is going on.'

Energised by his realisation that there might be more to the Captain's meander than we had previously thought, Eli began to walk faster, and I hurried to keep up. But when we reached the pub, there was no sign of the Captain. I wanted to stay with my large glass of wine and sit down until my toes healed, but Eli was restless.

'There's more to this, Daisy. Much more. He's up to something.' By the time he'd said this, or variations of it for about the thousandth time, I drained my glass and stood up.

'Come on then, where do we look next?'

'Everywhere,' Eli said.

I cursed my shoes. This was going to hurt.

Chapter Thirty-One

'Do you think we could narrow it down a bit? Before we go and try and walk every street in London looking for someone who apparently might or might not want to be found but certainly doesn't want to talk?'

'How do you suggest we do that?' There was an edge of exasperation in his voice, but he managed to keep it from becoming outright rudeness.

'Let me use the loo and I'll be able to think straight.'

'Good idea. I'll do the same and meet you back here in a minute.'

Eli made it back to the table before I did, and so I returned to find him staring at it. There, sat right in the middle, on a sticky black plastic tray, were two fresh glasses, one of wine and one a pint of cola. 'I thought we were heading off now?' I said, sitting down and taking a sip.

'Put it down,' Eli said, his voice low and serious. I wasn't used to him telling me what to do so I complied, but I raised an eyebrow at his tone. 'I didn't buy them. They were there when I got back from the bathroom.'

I sniffed my drink. 'It's the same wine that I was just drinking.'

'Someone's been watching us whilst we've been watching the Captain.'

A shiver ran down my spine. 'Someone who wants to help us or hurt us?'

'That's why I didn't want to touch them. When you're in the field, you don't eat or drink anything that could have been tampered with. As of now, we've got to act as though we're in hostile territory. Take precautions.'

I wrapped my arms around myself, feeling cold despite the ambient temperature which must have been at least in the mid-twenties. 'You're scaring me.'

Eli seemed to snap out of the highly tuned mode he'd been in and sat next to me. He pulled me against him, and I could feel his heart beat, slow and steady, underneath his thin polo shirt. It was soothing to realise that he was aware but not nervous about the situation. I tried to stay calm myself.

'We have to assume that someone is watching us. Don't turn around,' Eli cautioned, just as I was about to stand up and start staring at everyone in the place. There weren't many people. I tried to think back, without looking this time, to recall who had been there when we walked in. There had been a couple, out for a late lunch, probably from an office given his suit and her power shade of lipstick. They'd been too interested in each other to twang my radar then, or maybe that was their disguise? How did Eli go anywhere and not end up in a paranoid freak-out? I was struggling. I took a breath, calmed myself, thought back again.

There had been a biker, helmet at the floor by his feet as he sat alone at a tall table near the bar, shovelling a cheese sandwich and a pint of lemonade. I'd assumed him to be a courier, taking a break from deliveries and trying to rehydrate before braving the sunshine again in his leathers.

A young couple had been sat by the window. I'd wondered if they were old enough to drink legally. Not that they'd been paying any attention to their matching glasses of lager. They'd been deep in conversation about something displayed on the laptop in front of them. They were either playing an intense game or plotting to rule the world. They couldn't do a worse job than the leaders we currently had, and I had decided that they hadn't needed watching either.

Eli continued to stare at the glasses. 'I don't like it. Let's call Ben. He can track where we've walked on a map, see if there's anything that we missed.' He stood up and began to head to the door. I picked up the tray.

'I'll take this to the bar.' I always felt that I could tell a lot about my clients by spotting those who, like Mr King, finished their drinks and left the empties where they were, assuming that staff, obviously meaning me, would clear it for them. Whereas my favourite clients, like Arthur who came in every birthday, Christmas and Valentine's Day without fail to buy something for his wife of fifty years, always offered to wash up. I never let him, but it was the offer that counted. I often put aside an extra box of chocolates to slip into his bag as a little thank you.

As I lifted the tray, I spotted something underneath. 'Eli,' I called him back. 'These drinks were from the Captain.'

Eli returned to the table. 'How do you know that?'

'There's a postcard and a lottery ticket underneath. That's what you said he bought, in the shop?'

Eli didn't answer. He pulled his mobile out from his pocket, clicked off a couple of quick photos which I assumed he sent to my brother, then he reached for the card. 'Shouldn't you be wearing gloves?' I asked him. 'Just in case there are fingerprints?'

It was his turn to raise an eyebrow at me. 'What makes you think that our prints would show up in any database?' *Of course they wouldn't.* My brother would have seen to that. He glanced at the postcard, flipped it over, read something on the back and handed it to me. The picture on the front presumably gave us a location, on the back was a quick scrawl noting a time.

'I assume that this means he wants us to meet him at the London Eye at 4 p.m., but I've no idea what he means by "bring the lead".' I pronounced it as you would 'dog's lead'. 'Does it make any sense to you?'

Eli took it from me and read it once more. He glanced at his watch. 'We've got an hour to figure it out.' He tapped some more buttons on his phone. 'It'll take us an hour to walk there.' I groaned at the idea of walking that far in my sandals. The plasters were helping, but not enough to want to walk again just yet. 'It's quickest by tube, but we'd be stuck underground with no mobile reception and we're going to need Ben's help to figure this out in time. Does he need a lead for some equipment? A computer lead? I'll call a cab. We can speak to Ben en route.'

Chapter Thirty-Two

As the taxi stopped and started, crawling its way down Park Lane, we skirted the outside of a couple of the beautiful parks nestled right in the heart of London. I loved my city, for its historical buildings and its multicultural future-facing approach. New buildings crowded the skyline, but I ignored those and drank in the snatched glimpses of greenery hungrily.

Eli saw nothing but his phone screen. I surmised, given the scowl on his face and his occasional grunts, that he hadn't yet solved the puzzle about the lead. He glanced at his watch.

'Are we going to get there on time?' I asked him. 'What do we do when we get there? What if we can't work out what he wanted us to bring?'

'We'll get there fine,' Eli said, leaving unanswered the number of issues which wouldn't be so easily solved.

'Then why do you keep checking the time?' I asked. Also, drumming his fingers on the door handle and straightening the collar on his black polo shirt, his concession to pretending to be off duty.

'I was wondering whether we have time to stop and drop you at home, but I don't want to.'

'Careful. That almost sounded like you want me here working too,' I teased.

He stopped working on his phone for long enough to give my hand a quick squeeze. 'Would you be surprised to hear that I've actually enjoyed working with you today?'

'Very,' I told him, keeping hold of his hand. 'I know that it isn't easy for you to feel that I'm out in the field, but honestly, I don't think that you need to worry. I haven't walked anywhere that I wouldn't have gone myself at some point, probably with Lily.'

'Which could well have got you into worse trouble than a blister.'

'Quite probably.'

He fell silent and turned his attention back to his screen. I turned back to the window, people watching as we drove along. I kept waiting for the taxi driver to chip in; it was rare to get one who was as quiet as the man in front today. Usually by now we would have fielded a dozen questions about any holiday plans we had, or whether we had voted the same way as the cabbie on Brexit. After a few fraught journeys which had nearly come to me being kicked out in the middle of a journey, I had now learnt to ask first which way the driver had voted and then keep my mouth shut if I disagreed, just to get to my destination in one piece. It was a relief, though, that this one was giving us the time to think.

I looked at my own watch. We had forty minutes left before we were due to meet Jean-Luc again, and still no idea of what he needed us to bring. We were approaching the Park Lane Hilton, and I found myself daydreaming about how nice it would be, once all of this was over, to disappear with Eli for a few days to a hotel, with no-one else needing us, when a poster at the bus stop caught my eye.

I nudged Eli and pointed at it. 'Daisy, I'm trying to think. Whilst that poster does display a decent set of abs, I'm not Lily and really don't need to see them.'

I nudged him again. 'That's not why I got your attention. For a start, those abs are not as impressive as yours.' He managed a quick grin, and a wink. Considering the pressure he was under I was pleased that he still appreciated my loyalty. 'But also, it's an advert for perfume. Called Bear. Though he has a bare chest. B-E-A-R,' I spelled out, 'not B-A-R-E.'

'A-N-D,' Eli spelled back.

'Two words spelled differently but pronounced the same. What if Jean Luc meant a different pronunciation but spelled the same? Lead as in the metal, not as in a computer lead.' That thought earned me another kiss.

'I know exactly what he's asking for.' He rang Ben. 'I need you to pick up the suitcase prototype and meet me at the London Eye.'

'I take it that you're not concerned about Ben giving the game away anymore then, if you're asking him to come along too? You know he can't do covert. He stands out like a sore thumb everywhere except for universities and computer shops.'

'I just need the case,' Eli told me. 'After that he can go, and hopefully ...' he glanced yet again at his watch, '... he'll be home again before the Captain even shows up.' Having solved one puzzle, Eli turned his attention to the lottery ticket. 'Do these numbers mean anything to you?'

'Enough cash to buy a drink if he's matched three numbers, a place of our own if he's matched all six?' I suggested. That did not gain me any further affection.

'I've sent this to Ben. I've Googled it myself. I've added them, subtracted them and I've drawn a blank. Can you make another of your genius deductions?' he asked me.

But I couldn't, and was still staring at the piece of paper as we finally drew up by the river. Eli handed a bunch of notes to the driver. He didn't get a receipt and I wondered whether the Boss lady had a slush fund that she would use to supply him with more cash. There was a lot I didn't know about his job, and nothing so far that day encouraged me to want to get more involved.

The pavements seemed to have absorbed the heat of the day, and now radiated it back at us. I'd been glad of the wine when we had been in the pub, but the alcohol buzz had worn off, leaving me thirsty and with the beginnings of a headache. 'What now?' I asked Eli. 'The queue looks crazy long. I don't think we can buy tickets in time to get us on for four o'clock. Are we just supposed to wait around? See if he turns up again? What if this is a trap and we've just walked right into it?'

Chapter Thirty-Three

'If I'm right, and I understand what Jean-Luc was asking us to bring, then we're okay. But he isn't.' Eli had switched back into stealth mode, and though his dark eyes were now hidden behind his sunglasses, I sensed him sweeping his gaze over the crowd and absorbing every detail. He took up position at the edge of the path, next to a newly planted tree, his back to the wall and facing the Thames. He had taken possession of the case from Ben and sent my brother away again.

I took a look around too, as subtly as I could. I saw nothing. Lifting the camera to my eye, I looked again, much more slowly this time, as though I were framing shots. There were dozens of tourists around me doing the same thing, so there didn't seem to be any rush. It really was proving to be a useful cover after all.

An orange ribbon, held up by metal posts every couple of metres, guided the people queuing to snake around so that they were stood four lines deep on the pavement. Some faces were hidden behind maps or guidebooks. Some heads were covered in hats to protect the wearer from the glare of the sun, but in most cases I could make out enough, and rule out others by their height or gender. It was clear. The Captain was not among them.

'Sod it, you stay here and do whatever it is you do,' I told Eli. 'I'm going to score us some ice cream.'

Lily would have squealed or high-fived me for the suggestion. Eli gave a small nod, barely discernible from behind his own camera. 'Good to know I'm being useful again,' I muttered. That got his attention for long enough to put the camera down and give me a quick kiss on the cheek.

'Thank you,' Eli said. 'Take your time. I want to move

deeper into the crowds but it'll make me easier to spot if anyone is watching, and I don't want to put you in the cross hairs.'

As the thought of someone literally lining us up in the sights of a gun sunk in, the hairs on my arms rose and became goosebumps. 'Is it worth it?' I asked Eli. 'The risks you take? Does it make that much of a difference that it's worth risking your life?'

'Mine, yes,' Eli responded. 'Last year Ben intercepted some messages online. Most agencies wouldn't have had a chance to decrypt them, but we have a secret weapon.'

'My brother.'

'These groups have been so effective in Europe over the last ten years or so because they've been operating as individual cells. We take one out, but they don't know anything about anyone else, so we've struggled to infiltrate and take out the deeper networks. But they got cocky. This one man, in London, he started talking to cells in Leeds, in Liverpool, in Glasgow. They had picked a date and were going to launch attacks simultaneously. Realistically, the death toll would have been high, but it wouldn't have brought the country to a halt. But the fear might have, and that's what they were hoping.'

'They wanted to escalate the tension? I don't understand. Why would they care how much what they did upset people? Surely they just want to do as much damage as possible?'

'They do, but the more of a split they cause between the rest of the population and the groups they claim to act on behalf of, the more they hope that their people will be ostracised, and then drawn to their cause. They're half right, they bring about more hatred and fear but mostly people just hate what they do. We're not seeing many increases in their active membership in this country. So they wanted to go bigger, bolder, louder.'

'And Ben helped stop it?'

'He decrypted their messages, we coordinated responses, organised raids. We took out levels of the organisation we didn't even know existed. The mission probably saved several hundred lives initially, but it also prevented waves of anti-immigration stories in the media. It stopped the increases in hate crime which would have followed. It meant that people weren't spat at and abused in the streets. I know how it feels, Daisy, I know what it's like to be judged because of the colour of my skin.'

'You are the best person I know,' I told him. 'The bravest and the kindest.'

'But if you didn't know me, if you were walking home from the pub and I passed you on the street, would you speed up? Walk away, or would you stop and chat if I asked you?'

'Honestly, I'd walk away. But I'd avoid any man that approached me. It's not personal. I've just had far too many experiences of creepy men when I've been walking on my own to feel safe.'

'And probably even more when you've been walking with Lily?'

'Except she carries a can of pepper spray, sometimes wears shoes with a hidden blade in the heel and remembers far more from those self-defence classes that you made us take than I do.' I leant forward and kissed him quickly, then pulled him towards me and kissed him more deeply. 'I love you, Eli.'

'I love you too, now please can I get a mint choc-chip ice cream? And don't eat it all on the way back.'

I left him staring at the crowds, as I wandered away with a mind spinning with all of the issues we had talked about and dozens more that we hadn't, and cravings for ice cream that were getting stronger by the minute. I was surrounded in the queue by little people and their harassed keepers, discussing, arguing, threatening and bribing with promises of treats to keep the peace or to secure them one last item on their to-see list before they returned home, exhausted.

I gave way, allowing a particularly stressed looking woman with two children, a girl begging for an ice cream with a flake, and sauce, and as much additional sugar on top as it was possible to balance, and a boy, slightly younger from the look of him and deeply entrenched in the *Star Wars* universe, clutching a light saber in one hand and a Darth Vader mask in the other. The boy wanted an apple, but when the kiosk couldn't supply this he was satisfied with an ice lolly that was nearly as tall as he was. Finally, I made it to the front of the queue.

'Two mint choc-chips please.' I handed over some cash, tucked my purse back into my rucksack and pulled the top closed, hurrying to be ready in time to have my hands free to take the cones. I managed, and had thirty seconds spare to grab a handful of napkins and stuff them into my pocket too.

Carrying my prizes back to Eli, I licked the green liquid that dripped from the top and slid its way down the cone towards my hands. Eli took his, and managed to eat it without dropping a single glob. By contrast, I finished with sticky goo all over my fingers.

'Can you reach into my pocket and take a tissue out?' I asked Eli. 'There's a bottle of water in my bag. If you wet it I can clean up here.'

Eli did as I asked, but instead of pulling out the napkins, he produced two tickets to take a flight on the big wheel in just a few minutes' time.

Chapter Thirty-Four

'How the hell did he sneak those into my pocket without me noticing?' I asked Eli, for approximately the hundredth time since we had joined the snake-like queue.

'I assume that you had your mind on the ice cream and he could have got away with virtually anything,' Eli teased. His tone was light, but I could tell from looking at him how tense his body was.

We shuffled forward a few steps. I counted the people in front of us and consulted the guidebook I'd bought after we found the tickets. 'The pods can take twenty-five people at a time. We should make it into the next flight.'

'Flight? This is just a giant fun-fair ride. And a slow motion one at that. How long does it say it takes to do one circuit?'

'About half an hour,' I told him.

'Then we'll either have plenty of time to talk, assuming the Captain shows up, or ...'

'Or?'

'It's a trap and we're going to be locked in a glass bubble in range of half of London for the next thirty minutes.'

'When you say 'range'?'

'The target area of a decent sniper,' he added, helpfully. I gulped. He began to point out the windows of various buildings which faced us. 'Any of those would do it.'

'How do you leave the house in the morning?'

We reached the front of the queue and handed our tickets to the attendant in her red branded T-shirt. 'I see you've booked the champagne service and a private flight. Just so that you know, next time you could have skipped the queue and come straight to the VIP entrance.'

Eli swore under his breath, but I felt relieved. It was

hardly likely that Jean-Luc would have booked us a glass of champers if he was going to have us shot halfway round, unless this was his way of softening the blow.

The attendant didn't seem worried by our being in the wrong place and was utterly bemused at our shock about being shepherded on by ourselves when there was a line of probably at least another hundred people behind us. I wanted to apologise to them, but the pod door was open and Eli was waiting for me to join him. I climbed aboard and crossed straight to the far side to gaze out of the window. At ground level, I had a decent view of the river, packed with boat loads of tourists. There were only a few days a year when the weather really justified the use of the open-top boats, and the decks were crammed with people making the most of their good fortune. When we reached the apex we'd have the most amazing view. For a second I forgot that we had been sent here and just enjoyed being there with Eli.

The feeling faded as the door clanged shut and I turned towards the noise, only to come face to face with Eli and the Captain. Jean-Luc had somehow found himself a staff T-shirt, a tray and a bottle of champagne with three glasses. He set the tray down on the bench in the middle of the pod and gestured at the case by Eli's feet. No-one said a word.

Eli spun the combination locks until the numbers lined up, opened the box as though it were a regular briefcase, and waited until Jean-Luc had placed his mobile phone inside and closed the lid.

'Okay,' he said, once it was secured, 'may I offer you a glass of champagne? I, for one, could do with a little drink.' His accent was lush. I smiled at him, and Eli rolled his eyes at me.

'I could cope with a drink,' I said.

'Not for me, no alcohol when I'm working. I assume that we are actually working here?'

Jean-Luc bent his head and gave Eli a small bow. 'I have come to ask for your help.'

Eli scoffed. 'You led us on a wild goose chase. We walked half-way round the city trying to find you. If this is how you ask for a favour, I'd hate to think how you treat people that you don't need to use.' Eli took a step towards him. I felt like I was stuck in a pen with two studs about to do battle.

'Eli, Captain Jean-Luc, I'm sure we can find a way to talk about this.' I looked out of the window. We were maybe a third of the way around the circuit. 'We've got about twenty minutes and I suggest that we use them. And that you pour me a glass of champagne whilst you talk.'

'I take it that your brother came up with my nickname? Send my regards to Ben when you see him, please. I take it as a compliment that he calls me after the *Star Trek* captain. He is an intelligent and principled character, and in real life the actor is a great man. And thank your brother for this.' He gestured at the case, before pouring himself a glass of champagne and downing it. 'I am not worthy of the name.' His gorgeous voice rolled the rrrr's and rumbled its way from deep in his chest. If Eli hadn't been staring at him still, I could have melted for him. 'My compatriots would think me a philistine for drinking their champagne and not taking the time to savour it.' Had Lily been there she would doubtless have made comments along the lines of him savouring her. I was tempted, but Eli would not have found it funny.

'Can we cut to the chase? We have about eighteen minutes left.' Eli was definitely not enjoying his company as much as I was.

'They have my girlfriend,' the Captain said. 'Natalya, they took her two weeks ago. I waited to get their demands, but there were none, only a ticket to London and the name of a hotel to check into.'

'And this gave you the idea to set us up with this waste of time?' Eli asked.

'Forgive me.'

'I do,' I said.

'Daisy …' Eli muttered from between gritted teeth.

'When I landed, I was handed a mobile phone and told to keep it switched on all the time. They've had me walking round London, and two days ago I finally found out why. They're a new organisation, they weren't on my radar and I doubt that they are on yours. They want to launch a series of attacks on London, which they'll blame on immigrants from Eastern Europe. The media will have a field day.'

'And your phone?' I asked the Captain.

'They breached the security features on it. They've been switching the camera and microphone on the phone at random to check up on me. I couldn't run the risk that they'd hear me if I spoke to you without it being in Ben's briefcase. They're using me to scout locations for them so I have an excuse to be here. They want my face captured on CCTV so that they can claim that governments across the continent are also implicated. Before I left, they made huge payments in my name so I look like I have been compromised, paid off my mortgage, I only found out when I got a letter from my bank. I'm hoping that they'll stop checking for a few minutes whilst I'm on here and not notice that my phone won't connect. They'll expect a report on the security weaknesses of the tourist site however, they've had me scope out several others already in a similar way. It will aid their agenda to foster distrust on all sides. Ben mentioned this case last time I saw him. I knew it meant we could finally talk but I couldn't think of a safe way to ask you to bring it. I didn't want them to know that we were meeting. That's why I was trying to get your attention in the office. Your colleagues, Ben aside, they are not quick. I stood there for three days before I could find a way to get you away from the office. Hopefully if you help me bring them down, we can fix up any weaknesses in your team that they were hoping to exploit.'

'I'll do my best,' Eli promised.

'And the lottery ticket?' I asked.

'A string of numbers I heard them mention. I don't know what they mean. Have you managed to decipher it yet?'

Eli swore. 'I'll ring Ben and see if he's had any brain waves.

Chapter Thirty-Five

'It's a location,' Ben said, as Erin placed a giant tray of aubergine moussaka on the table. Dad had made it but then announced that he was taking his and Cody's portions to eat at her house. He was a wise man. I wasn't sure that I wanted to be sat in the room either. The tension was palpable.

'Took me a few minutes, at first I wondered whether it was bank accounts, but nothing showed up. It turns out, if you take them as three sets of coordinates, you get a field outside of Epping.'

Eli passed around plates and Erin sliced a homemade stick of garlic bread. Ben ignored them and cleared a space of cutlery to put his laptop on the table. 'Here.' He showed us an aerial map.

'It's very ... green,' I said. Ben clicked a few more buttons, and the view zoomed in until we could make out a dirt track and a tumbledown barn. 'How sure are you that this is where they meant?' I asked. 'The Captain said he heard them mentioning the numbers but even he didn't know what they referred to.'

I shouldn't have worried. Ben would have checked ownership details, tax bills and legal documents until he was sure. 'I've sent this to the Boss, but she doesn't want to risk putting an official team together. If the Captain is implicated, it could be embarrassing to our French partners. She would prefer that Eli and Taylor handle it. Discreetly.'

Eli pulled his mobile out and dialled Taylor's number. They had a rapid conversation which seemed to quickly descend into jargon and acronyms. I couldn't follow half of it, except for the bit where they seemed to decide that the two of them would be enough to mount a raid.

I waited until they had finished. I wanted to ask Eli what

he was thinking, planning to go up against a group capable of manipulating even the security of an expert such as the Captain, with only Taylor to help him? It wasn't as if he even liked or trusted Taylor. I tried to catch his eye to talk, but he kept his gaze down, focused on his plate, so I waited.

Erin had made a salad, and Ben had copied one of Dad's famous chocolate cake recipes, so the meal seemed to last forever. The peace treaty which Erin and I had unofficially declared during our stay in the spa was holding, and I tried my best to be polite, even though all I wanted was to drag Eli outside and ask him why on earth he was planning to do something so dangerous.

When Eli offered to wash up afterwards, I nearly screamed. Thankfully Ben turned him down. He had high standards and was never sure that anyone else could live up to them, so he was often happy to volunteer to do the pots himself. I thanked him, took Eli by the hand and pulled him downstairs. As I shut the door behind us, marking our safe return to the notional privacy of my flat, I finally had the space to share my thoughts.

'What the hell are you thinking? You and Taylor cannot possibly be planning to go there on your own to rescue the Captain's girlfriend. It isn't safe.'

Eli put his finger gently against my lips. I might have been sharing my thoughts a little louder than even I had planned to. 'Daisy, it'll be fine. We're professionals.' He lifted his hand and placed his lips against mine instead, but I wasn't going to be distracted so easily.

'You don't act like it. You second guess everything Taylor suggests normally. There is no way you trust him enough to go on a mission like this alone with him. I've listened to how worried you were when Lily and I offered to help you out in the past. I've taken the self-defence classes that you asked me to, I stay out of your business as much as I can. Now it's your turn to afford me the same courtesy. Now

I'm sorry that Jean-Luc's girlfriend is in trouble, and I know that she needs our help, but I am asking you, in fact, I am begging you, please don't do it like this. Let's talk to your Boss; surely she can find a couple more people to go with you. Hell, I'd rather go with you than have you go in short-handed. Surely that makes the whole thing a hundred times more dangerous. You told me that you were scared of losing me. Well, I'm terrified of losing you. You are my strength and my comfort. My best friend, my partner, my love. I know how it feels to be lonely and grieving, how it feels to drag yourself out of bed and not know how you are going to get through the day because everything feels pointless without having the people you love to share it with. I've seen my dad almost break with the pain. I don't ever *ever* want to go through the same by losing you.'

By the time I finished, tears were dripping down my face. My skin was red, and my shoulders were shaking with the adrenaline coursing through me. Eli pulled me into him, wrapped his arms around me and held me as I sobbed into his chest.

'You won't lose me.'

'You can't promise me that.'

'I can promise that I love you, and I will always love you,' Eli said, cupping my cheek in his hand as gently as you would hold a baby bird. He placed a kiss on my lips, and another on my forehead. I stood on tiptoes and reached up to kiss him back.

We fell into bed, trying to show each other physically how deep our affection ran, and afterwards Eli held me, and we fell asleep tangled in each other's arms. But when I woke up, he was gone.

Chapter Thirty-Six

I rang Lily. 'Is Taylor with you?'

'Good morning to you too. What time is it?' She went quiet for a second, probably looking at her clock. 'Jeez, Daisy, what time do you call this? I didn't get out of work until two. We were having a sale on our DVDs, making space for a shipment of leather goods my manager got in a closing down sale. I brought a couple of things home to test with Taylor, and I was counting on a bit more sleep.' She yawned so loudly that I had to pull the handset from my ear.

'And Taylor?'

'Seemed to enjoy them. He looked a bit nervous when I pulled out the—'

'—is he there?' I interrupted.

'No. He said he had to go to work. Doesn't Eli know where he is?'

I had a horrible feeling that Eli knew exactly where he was. I apologised for waking Lily and hung up. There was no point in both of us worrying. Lying down and pulling the duvet back up to my chin, I tried to relax but it was no use. It was bad enough when I had no idea what Eli was up to. It was torture waiting when I knew that he was doing something not only dangerous, but probably also fairly stupid.

Shoving the covers off, I got out of bed, tugged on a pair of jeans that were lying on the floor and made for the stairs. Erin and Ben were sat at Dad's kitchen table, digging in to matching bowls of muesli. I wasn't sure how Erin had managed to persuade him to move on from the cocoa puffs he had eaten every day since he was six, goodness knows that Dad and I had never managed to.

'Do you know where Eli is?' I asked them.

Erin immediately stood up and began to tidy the already spotless kitchen. Ben ignored me and continued to eat without looking up.

'Ben.' I raised my voice, not loud enough to upset him, but enough to let him know that I was serious and wanted his attention. He looked up. 'Your Boss has decided that she places a greater importance on relations with the French office than the lives of two of her own team,'

I saw Ben swallow nervously, and I tried to temper my words. 'Eli assures me that he'll be okay, but it can't be safe, surely? There's two of them and goodness knows how many on the other side. There must be something I can do? I promised Eli that I wouldn't take any risks, but he can't or won't afford me the same security. I have to help him.'

'He won't thank you if you try, Daisy,' Ben warned.

'I know, but I have to go. Now, you cracked the coordinates that were on the lottery ticket. Where has Eli gone? I won't take any stupid risks, I promise, but you need to tell me where they are.'

'I can't,' Ben said. He began wringing his hands. It was a sure sign that he felt under pressure, and whilst I wanted to stop and let him calm down, Eli was in danger and for once I didn't have time to spare trying to protect my brother.

'Tell me,' I demanded.

'Please don't make me.' He stopped wringing his hands and instead covered his ears and closed his eyes. I hated what I was doing to him. If it had been anyone except my Eli out there, I would have let my brother be.

'Ben, I'm begging you.'

'Daisy, I think you need to leave.' Erin stepped in front of me, and whilst I hated her for standing in the way of me reaching Eli, I loved seeing how she was protecting my brother. She took my arm and guided me towards the stairs down to my flat. I tried to twist my arm away from her, but she was surprisingly strong. Mind you, she'd probably needed to be to cart Ben onto the ferry the year before. As I pulled my arm free, she grabbed for my hand. I snatched it away, but not before I felt a scrap of paper pass from her palm to mine. 'Go,' she told me. 'Quickly.' Her tone had changed, but Ben wouldn't have noticed it. I did.

As I got downstairs, I unfolded the note to find an address and postcode.

I opened the map app on my phone and entered the details. The farm was about twenty miles away, and I'd be able to do most of that by train, but the last bit was going to involve more cross-country running than I had done since secondary school. I crossed my fingers that it wouldn't kill me before I even got close. I pulled on socks and trainers and hoped that my sandal-related injuries wouldn't slow me down too badly.

I was just locking the door behind me when I heard a cough. Turning around, I found Mr King. He was stood next to his gleaming Jaguar and was slowly removing his leather driving gloves. Quite why he needed them when it hadn't been cool enough to need any additional layers in weeks, I had no idea.

'I'm sorry,' I told him. 'I've got an emergency and the shop won't be open this morning.'

'Anything I can do to help?'

'Not really. This is …' How to explain what Eli did without giving the game away? 'I can't talk about it, but suffice to say that it's really very important and I'm sorry that I don't have time to find you the perfect gift right now, but I have to go.' The last few words squeaked out past my grated teeth.

'Is it your fellow?' Mr King asked. 'I saw him on my way here. Looked to be in an awful hurry.'

I nodded. 'I need to help him and it's going to take me far longer to get where he's going than it'll take him.'

'I'll drive you. You've rescued me plenty of times recently. It would be my pleasure to help you.'

I wanted to take him up on his offer but I couldn't, not in all conscience. It wouldn't be safe and I couldn't tell him any of the details. 'I can't drag you into this,' I told Mr King.

'Nonsense. I served in Her Majesty's Army for twenty years before I joined my bank. There's nothing you could be involved in that would be more dangerous than what I've been through before.'

I hesitated. It was all the time Mr King needed to know I was tempted by his offer after all.

'Jump in.' He asked where we were going and typed the address into the sat-nav embedded in the control panel. 'I suggest that you fasten your seatbelt.' I did as he said and found that, despite the tension, it was hard not to relax into the plush leather seats. 'I must say I've missed the adrenaline of a good chase,' he said, shifting the gears effortlessly as he accelerated and we started our journey to find Eli.

Chapter Thirty-Seven

It always amazed me how quickly it was possible to leave the concrete haven of my city and be out in the countryside. It felt as though no time at all had passed since we had left my flat, and yet it still seemed to be taking far too long to reach Eli. Mr King drove smoothly, but fast. The car was sleek and it glided through the miles. Before long, we were speeding down main roads with fields on either side and I was staring out the window trying to spot the turning we needed.

'I won't miss it,' Mr King assured me. I sat back. His confidence was so assured that I found myself sitting back in my seat. 'Ten more minutes,' he announced. 'Perhaps now would be a good time for you to enlighten me as to the plan.'

'Plan, yes, we should definitely make one of those.'

If Mr King was surprised, he was too polite to show it. 'What were you aiming to achieve by meeting up with your partner?'

'I just wanted to check that he was okay.' Even to my ears that sounded pathetic. 'He's in a situation and I don't think he has enough back-up, but he won't want me to get close. I wanted to be nearby, in case I could help, but I hadn't really worked out how.'

'Then might I suggest we take a quick pass by the address you gave me? We can assure ourselves that all is well. I'll have you back behind your shop counter by lunchtime.' It sounded so simple when he said it, and I found myself nodding. 'I'm sure once you see that everything is under control you will be quite satisfied.' I could only hope that he was correct.

'Turn left in three hundred yards.' I jumped at the sound of the sat-nav directing us to leave the main road and wind our way into the countryside.

'Hopefully we'll be able to see what we need from the car,' I said.

'What are you hoping to find?'

'Nothing,' I told him. 'Hopefully, absolutely nothing. If all is well Eli and his colleague will be staying under the radar. They won't need us, and I'll never need to tell him that we were here.'

'He's not expecting you?'

'He'd be devastated if he knew that I was taking any risks. He's not being sexist, he's just scared that I'll get hurt.'

'A little old-fashioned chivalry never hurt anyone.'

I wasn't sure. I thought that the behavioural constraints thinly disguised as protection for my gender nominally for the sake of our safety had held us back from education and many jobs for hundreds of years, but now wasn't the time to argue. I needed him to get me closer to Eli. I'd try and find some way to unpick the issues in his beliefs another time.

'There,' I said, pointing as we passed the barn that Ben had showed us the day before on the satellite.

It sat several fields back from the main road. Its wooden sides had seen better days, and there were large gaps where boards had come loose over the years. The tiled roof was no more structurally sound. I began to doubt that this could ever have been used as a base, but then I remembered that it was Ben who had located it, and that I therefore had no basis for my distrust. My brother was frequently out of sync with the people around him but rarely wrong when it came to his job.

We passed a lane which looked as though it led towards the barn, but Mr King didn't take it. I was about to question him when he indicated right and took the next dirt track instead. The Jag's suspension wasn't up to the challenge posed by the pot holes, and we bounced around in our seats.

'I'm sorry, I hope that this doesn't damage your beautiful car.'

'I'm sure this lady can handle anything we ask of her,' he replied, giving the dashboard an affectionate pat. He was smiling.

'Are you enjoying this?' I asked.

'Given that the alternative was a briefing by one of my more verbose colleagues about proposed new tax laws and was scheduled to last for three hours, I'm very happy to be here.'

'I can't guarantee that this is a hundred percent safe,' I cautioned.

'Then it is lucky I never asked you to.' He pressed the accelerator again and the engine purred under his foot, speeding us on, past the barn until he came to another path which ran behind it. He drove until we reached the end of the lane, where he performed a neat three-point turn and left us pointing back towards the road in case we needed to leave in a hurry.

I looked at the sat-nav display. It showed our location in the middle of a green square. The voice kept asking us to double back and take the next left, but thankfully it didn't get ever more frustrated as we ignored it. If only my dad had displayed the same patience when he had to chase me and Ben around to get ready for school all of those years before.

Our view of the barn was impeded by a small thicket of trees that weren't evident on the display. 'I'm going to get a little closer,' I told Mr King.

Chapter Thirty-Eight

'You can wait in the car,' I said, for at least the tenth time.

'Not a chance. I haven't had this much fun in decades. Now, how many hostiles are we expecting?'

He asked it as though they were guests at a party. 'No idea,' I told him. 'Eli thought that he and Taylor would be okay, so I guess not many. I just couldn't sit at home waiting for him to return and keeping my fingers crossed.'

'I was always happiest when I was in the thick of things.' The twigs and leaves crunched under the soles of his spotless Oxford brogues. We reached the outskirts of the proto-forest on the edge of the field.

'I suggest that we wait here,' I said. There was no noise coming from the barn, no scent of gunpowder or fear, except for my own. 'I don't have any breakfast, I'm afraid,' I said, digging into my bag and drawing out a box of cereal bars, 'but I've got these, and there are a couple of bottles of water in here somewhere.'

'Thank you,' Mr King said, taking one and handing me back the box.

'This isn't my first stake-out. Now, I've got binoculars, crossword puzzles and a she-pee, though I suspect I'll find that more useful than you will.' We found a tree trunk which had fallen at some point, providing a convenient place to sit. We waited. Nothing happened.

'Are you sure we have the correct location?' Mr King asked, finally. I didn't blame him. We'd been there for an hour and not so much as a pigeon had flown overhead.

'We do. Perhaps they didn't need us after all. If it's still this calm, maybe they've been ...' I was about to add '... and gone,' but a shot rang out and shattered the peace.

'Down!' yelled Mr King, and we threw ourselves behind

the log. 'It seems,' he said, in between catching his breath and breaking out into another rare smile, 'that we are in the correct place after all.'

'Stay here,' I told him. 'I'm going to get a bit closer.' There was no cover, save for the long grass, grown yellow and dry from the lack of recent rain. I crouched down, glad for once of my mousy hair which would act as a perfect camouflage. Crawling forward, I inched my way closer and closer to the barn.

There were no more shots, and as I cleared the patch of wildflowers, I began to feel more confident. Rising to my feet, I hid behind the final tree as I began to plan my approach. I was going to zig-zag my way across the open grass and flatten myself against the side of the barn. In a movie, that would have been where I would have drawn my weapon, but in real life I had nothing except a nail file and an overwhelming desire to protect Eli.

I took a couple of deep breaths to prepare myself for the flat-out run I'd have to do to try and make it across the patch with no cover before anyone spotted me. I gave myself a countdown. Ten. Breathe. Nine. Pick the spot I was aiming at. Eight. Check my shoelaces were tied. Seven. Draw in as much oxygen as I could. Six. Tie my hair back so that it didn't obstruct my view. Five. Try to ignore my heart which was beating so hard it felt like it was going to break free from my chest. Four. Wring my hands. Three. Any second.

Another shot rang out, breaking the silence and sending a flock of crows scattering with a chorus of disgruntled squawks.

Eli.

My heart thumped. I ran.

Reaching the edge of the building, I hunched down and panted, trying to catch my breath. Once I could hear again over the sound of my breathing I lent in and put my ear against a crack in the wood. There were no sounds from inside. No more shots, but no talking either. I tried to peek through the gap, but it was too small to see anything but shadows.

I was trying to decide what to do next, whether to head back to the relative safety of the car or to stay close just in case Eli needed help. I looked back over my shoulder to glance at Mr King. He was sheltered by the log; I could just see the top of his head poking out from over the top. As I watched he raised himself so that he could see over the wood. We made eye contact and he gave me a thumbs up. I was glad someone wanted to be there.

Turning back to the hut, I crept round the edge, keeping one ear to the building at all times. I was about to give up and head back to meet Mr King when I heard banging. It wasn't more shots, but it wasn't exactly a good noise either. I reached the door. It was time to decide. Go in and risk making Eli angry if all was well, or leave him, underprepared and without adequate back-up to face whoever was inside?

Another bang, loud enough to send plumes of dust drifting through the cracks, made my decision for me. The old metal hinges squeaked, despite how gently I was trying to ease them. I swore under my breath. Would it be best to open the door rapidly and burst in, just in case they heard the noise, or go slowly and hope they didn't notice? I heard Eli's voice, clearer now that there was a few inches of space at the side of the door.

'Put the gun down. You're outnumbered and we've got back-up on the way.' He was trying to bluff – the only other person who could help him now was me – but why was he doing so? If things were going his way, he wouldn't need to lie.

I lay on my belly and crawled through the dirt, inching my way through the door and further into the barn. There was a wooden barrier carving the barn into two compartments.

The one I was in was empty but for a few old hay bales around the right wall, left to spoil.

I heard Eli again. His voice seemed to be coming from just the other side of the divider. 'You won't get away. We've got four of your co-conspirators so we'll know who you are and I will personally track you down and kill you.' There was a cold edge to his voice that I wasn't used to hearing. I believed him, and I'd only ever known him being gentle. The other guy ought to be bloody terrified.

Another voice. This one with a French accent, but not the Captain. 'You say this but I'm the one with the gun. So it seems the advantage is mine, no?'

Damn. Eli really was in trouble. I had no idea where Taylor or the Captain were and could only hope that they hadn't been harmed by the shots I'd heard earlier. I continued to crawl as the dust got in my hair and up my nose. I paused to rub my face against my sleeve. If I sneezed now, I'd blow any chance I had of helping Eli.

The divider wall ran three quarters of the width of the barn, and I'd been safely hidden by it for most of my journey from the door, but to see what was happening on the other side I would need to reach it and then go round it, at which point I too would likely be in the direct line of sight of the person holding the gun.

I looked around to see if there was anything I could use. An old rusty bucket, it's bottom more hole than metal sat forgotten in one corner. An old broom in another. Neither would help me now. If only Lily was there with her trusty handbag full of surprises. I'd left my handbag in the car and of course there were no handy pockets in my outfit, so I had just my wits and lack of experience to help me. We were screwed.

'At least tell me why you took Natalya.' That was Eli. He was trying to sound confident but I could hear the waver in his voice. He was stalling for time. I inched forward some more and felt something hard under my hip. Searching in the dirt, my fingers dug out an old bicycle chain. Better than nothing.

A few more metres and I was close to the divider, still hidden by it, but not for much longer. I reached it and climbed to my knees, then my feet. I took a tentative step, flinching when I heard the muck crunch and compact under my shoes.

'What was that?' The accent again.

'It's an old barn, bound to be a few creaks.' That was Taylor, so he was still there. Was he being held at gunpoint too? If not, why hadn't he rescued Eli already? Something was desperately wrong.

I weighed the chain in my hands. It wasn't heavy, but it was long. I swung it, getting a feel for it in my hands. I was two steps from the end of the wooden divide.

'Where was I? Oh yes, I'm going to shoot you and then I'll kill both your friends.'

That was all I needed to hear. I took the last few steps at speed, swinging the chain around my head. As I cleared the divider and caught sight of the other half of the barn, I saw Eli on his knees in the centre. A gun was pointed at his head. I set my sights on the man holding it and tossed the chain at him with a fury I'd never felt before.

He saw me, just at the last second and ducked to his left. He wasn't quick enough. The metal caught his cheek. He fell forward, and one last shot rang out. I screamed.

Eli tumbled forward. I ran to him, grabbed him and traced my hands over his face, his chest. I kissed him and held him and kissed him again.

Taylor sprang to his feet, drew a pair of handcuffs from his back pocket and began to fasten them around the shooter's wrists, not that he looked as though he would be fit to go anywhere any time soon. My aim had been true; he had a large gash on one cheek and appeared to be unconscious.

'You're okay?'

'Bastard shot me in the leg. What the hell are you doing here?'

'Saving your life, it seems. I was scared you didn't have enough back-up. I was right. What happened?' I asked, as we guided him to sit up. I rolled up his trouser leg, pausing as he winced.

'Someone had got there before we did.'

'Was it a set-up? Were they waiting for you?' I tried to rip a length off my shirt to use as a bandage but the material was stronger than I was and held firm.

Eli drew a sharp breath in over his teeth as I slipped my blouse off and used it to try and stem the bleeding. 'No, I don't think so. We found five of the gang we believe were setting the Captain up.'

'What's going on?' Mr King appeared from around the divider. 'Did we get here in time?'

The white fabric pressed against Eli's skin had turned a disconcerting shade of pink. I gestured to Mr King. 'Your tie, please, I need to stop the bleeding. We did, thanks to you.'

He loosened the knot, slipped it off and handed it to me. I wrapped it around Eli's leg, a few inches above the wound in his calf and pulled it tight. Lifting the blouse, I was relieved to see that the flow had slowed to a trickle. Eli took the fabric from me, folded it to find a patch that wasn't as soggy as the rest and replaced it.

'I don't think it was anyone in their gang who got here before us. They'd have no reason to leave a bunch of men tied up, gagged and locked in a make-shift cell. It was weird, it felt like we were walking into a clean-up stage of an operation, not the raid we were expecting. I think we lowered our guard too much.'

'Did the Captain get here before you?'

'No, we picked him up on our way here. It was a risk, when someone is emotionally compromised they're less reliable, but we needed the extra body.' He lifted the cloth and peeked underneath it again.

Emotionally compromised. Was that Eli's way of explaining how he felt when he thought I was in danger? It was a cold term for the desperate fear that had punched me in the gut when I had seen Eli emerge in pain. 'Is Taylor alright keeping an eye on them? I'm assuming your Boss will send in a containment team now you've got them all?'

Eli nodded. 'Taylor's okay. But we were right about the Captain. He took one of the prisoners out of the cell to question him. Removed his gag, loosened the ropes he'd been tied up in so that he could try and beat the information out of him. But he was distracted, too close to the situation. The guy got an arm free, grabbed his gun and that's when you arrived. I wanted Taylor to take the shot, but he wasn't confident he could take the man out without hitting me. He was getting closer to risking it though. Honestly, I think if you'd been much longer you'd have been wiping bits of one of us off the barn walls. Hopefully his and not mine.'

I heard a sob and realised that it had come from me. Eli drew me against him again and kissed me.

Mr King held out a hand for Eli to shake. 'Major King, retired. I was popping in to Daisy's wonderful boutique to thank her for her work and pass on an additional payment for the successful event. Daisy was concerned that you were short-staffed and it seems to me that she was correct.'

'Believe it or not, I'm very glad that you're here,' Eli told me.

'Did you find Natalya?' I asked.

'There's no sign. The Captain is tearing the place apart but I'm not sure he's calm enough to decipher any clues should he find them. I need to help.'

'You need to go to a hospital, young man.'

Eli ignored Mr King and struggled to his feet. 'The bleeding has stopped.'

'For now.' Mr King didn't look happy at the idea of him going back to work either.

'You said they were all tied up when you arrived,' I said, my brain finally accepting that Eli was safe and beginning to function again. 'There must be someone else here on our side. How else could they have been restrained before you started?'

Chapter Thirty-Nine

Eli must have been in agony because he didn't have an answer. His skin had taken on a grey pallor and beads of sweat lined his forehead, but he gritted his teeth and gave no other indication of it.

The barn was dim, but for the rays of sunshine which broke through where the tiles had slipped, leaving holes in the roof. It gave the shadows a patchy appearance. Not enough sun had made it through to warm the air, and I shivered.

In what looked to be a tumbledown stable in one corner of the barn, the impressive figure of Taylor stood over a cowering group of smaller men. In the shadows, I could hear but not see the signs of a search. Wood crashed against wood, and plumes of dust whirled their way across the air towards us, spiralling in the few areas which we could see.

Eli crossed towards Taylor. He slapped him on the back, and I knew that when things had quietened that this would mark a thaw in their relationship. For now though, there was no time to lose. 'I'm going to find the Captain. He's going to tear this place to pieces and I'm not sure the barn is stable enough to withstand it,' Taylor said.

Mr King pulled a lighter from his pocket. Clicking it on, I could see his face in the orange light it cast. He was smiling. 'I'll help.'

The back half of the room was in better shape. Here, the corner facing the stable had also been boxed in with sheets of plywood to create an office. I could see the Captain inside, lit by a portable electric lamp. He held sheaves of paper in his hands and a makeshift desk of old milk crates was covered in discarded mobile phones and laptops.

As we approached, he threw the papers to the floor,

dropped his head to his hands and his knees to the floor. My anger that his actions had put Eli in danger dissipated, and I ran to him. Pulling him against me and holding him, I told him 'We'll find her. Someone here is on our side, else why would they have left these men tied up for us to find?'

'How, Daisy? I've been through every file and piece of equipment in here. There is no sign of where they've taken her.'

'I'll call Ben. He can find files that they'll think they deleted that no-one else would ever see. He'll crack their phones and tell us every place they've been.'

The Captain looked up, and the lamp gave enough light that I could see the hope sparking again in his eyes. 'Tell Ben to hurry.'

I left Mr King and the Captain picking up the papers and devices and piling them into a crate for Ben to go through on his arrival. Evidently there were more that the Captain had scattered already, and they had armfuls by the time I reached the double doors at the side of the barn.

The front doors were stiff, and I had to shove them with my hip to get them to budge open. Outside the sunshine seemed brighter by comparison, and I found myself scrunching my eyes against the glare.

My phone had barely any signal, so I fired off a series of texts to Ben. They'd be more likely to get through and he'd understand the situation more than from a garbled phone call. His replies began to arrive before I had finished explaining, and I struggled to keep the thread straight in my head as I tried to reply to his questions at the same time as I asked whether he could arrange for anyone to come and help. The Boss may have wanted to keep the Captain's predicament quiet to begin with, but now that at least most of the gang had been subdued, surely there was enough evidence to clear him and let us get some back-up? Hopefully they would also be able to send healthcare for Eli, who by now must be feeling the effects of the gunshot wound. It would be agony after the adrenaline wore off.

Ben's final text seemed to indicate that someone was on the way, but he gave little detail as to who that might be. I asked him again and again, but he stopped replying. I rang but got no answer. Sadly, with Ben, there were no guarantees. He'd be perfectly capable of sending an entire IT department to go through the paperwork and laptops in the makeshift office but equally also assume that I'd look after Eli and neglect to send an ambulance. Should I call one myself? Or would bringing in outsiders compromise whatever operation was needed to try to locate and rescue Natalya?

The door behind me opened, and I was relieved when Eli emerged. He looked grey and was walking with a noticeable limp. His forehead was tense, giving him little lines that I'd never noticed before. 'Are you okay?' I asked.

'Not really. Getting shot isn't the best way to start my day.'

'Ben is sending help.'

'For the data or for the people?' Eli knew my brother as well as I did. He loved him too, despite Ben's idiosyncrasies. I loved Eli for how he had always supported, encouraged and protected my brother. I crossed to him and reached out for a hug. He held me against him, and I breathed him in, sensing his pain and the strength he was displaying to carry him through.

Eli needed to sit, but there were very few options. The yard in front of the barn was mostly a scarred patch of pot-holes and puddles. 'We're parked at the back, behind the woods. Shall we go to the car?'

Eli shook his head. 'I need to stay until more help arrives. Mr King is inside making sure that no-one else gets loose. Why did you never tell me he was so useful in a crisis?'

'Because he has never been anything other than a source of deep, deep stress to me until today.'

Eli winced. 'Perhaps sitting down would be a good idea. I don't suppose you have any heavy-duty painkillers in the car?'

'Only paracetamol I'm afraid.'

'Yeah, that's probably not going to cut this.' He leant against the wall of the barn, using one palm to support himself while he lifted his leg and used the other hand to look under the cloth. 'I was lucky. The bullet went straight through and missed the bone.'

My own reserves of adrenaline which had kept me sharp but also prevented me from thinking about the dangers that Eli had faced began to fade, and I started to shake. 'Daisy?' I heard Eli calling but couldn't respond. Suddenly the snacks that I had shared with Mr King earlier came back to haunt me. My stomach heaved, and I scanned the yard trying to find somewhere private where I could throw up.

There was a rickety wooden hut, smaller than a garden shed in the far corner. Hoping it contained a loo, I lurched across the ground, hands clamped to my mouth. The fifty or so metres felt more like five hundred as I hurried to get there before I lost all control of my stomach. Opening the door, I didn't spot what I had been hoping for, but it no longer mattered ...

Chapter Forty

'Eli,' I screamed. 'Eli!' Even though I knew he could hardly walk, let alone run. 'I've found her. I've got Natalya.' Behind me I heard Eli calling the Captain, and I wished that I had thought to tell him to wait. I reached for her, nervous that I was going to touch a dead body, she was lying so still. The Captain hadn't proved to be as calm in a crisis as Eli, and I worried that he would lash out if the worst had happened to her. I went to touch her shoulder. Though I'd hoped that she was alive I still jumped out of my skin when she stirred. I tried to talk to her, but my lousy French wasn't up to much explaining.

'*Ça va*?' I tried, straining my brain to recall whether I was asking if she was okay or telling her that it was okay. Nothing. I reached out to shake her arm gently to see if I could wake her up more.

The next thing I knew, I was lying on my back on the ground, her arm wrapped around my neck, as she held me in a choke position. '*Ça va bien*,' she replied, which couldn't be right because I thought that '*bien*' meant good, and there was nothing good about her half killing me, except that it meant that she was alive.

'Natalya!' The Captain came running. She let go of my neck, and I drew in grateful breaths now that my windpipe was no longer constricted.

Eli finally joined us, favouring his left leg heavily. He sank down on the ground next to me, and we held each other. 'Are you okay?' he asked.

'Less dinged up than you are. That just took me by surprise. One second I was trying to see if she was alive, the next she had thrown me judo style and was cutting off my oxygen.'

'I apologise,' Natalya said, letting go of the Captain and coming to check on me. 'I thought I had subdued all of them, I came in here hoping to use the lavatory, they only gave me a bucket, but I haven't eaten for two days and I passed out.' Her English was excellent, better than mine probably but with a beautiful accent. Eli seemed rapt.

'Aren't you supposed to be in pain?' I asked him.

'I'm trying to take my mind off it.'

I ignored his grin and turned back to Natalya. 'Are you okay? Did they hurt you?'

'*Non.* They thought that I would be too scared to be any trouble. They hoped to use my presence to ensure that Laurent would do as they requested.'

The Captain, Laurent to give him his proper name, was grinning at her now. 'They didn't count on her being a skilled operative also.'

'Serves them right for underestimating women,' I said. 'But why did they take her?'

'They thought they could use us to find out how to replace the weapons that were captured in Ben's raid. I think they were desperate,' the Captain explained to me.

We didn't get a chance to talk again, as Ben's help crew arrived. First to emerge from the muddy jeep was the Boss lady. She congratulated us on a successful mission, assigned the two men who followed her out of the vehicle to guard the suspects and began a rapid fire exchange with Natalya in French. I was lost as soon as they got past '*bonjour*', so I concentrated on Eli, as no-one else seemed to be.

'Now can we get you to a hospital?' I said. He agreed, and I hurried inside to update Mr King and ask one more favour of him.

'But just how are we going to explain him turning up with a hole in his leg?' Mr King asked, before leaving to fetch his car.

He drove the loop which brought him in as close to the

barn as he could get. Eli thanked him. The fact that he hadn't protested and insisted that he would walk across the field to the car was a sign of how much discomfort he was in. 'Usually we use fake armed forces ID and claim that it was a live fire training exercise,' he said.

'How often do people get shot that you have an excuse that "usually" gets used?'

The nurse at the front desk was shocked to see a gunshot wound. I was reassured by her response that it was normal to find the whole situation unsettling. Now that Eli was set up in a cubicle, hooked up to a drip and a stonking supply of painkillers he looked better and his sense of humour was definitely restored.

'Daisy, can you see if you can grab a couple more chairs?' Eli asked, as Ben, Erin, my dad and Cody all arrived at once to check on him.

'Okay, but I don't think they're going to like it.' The doctor had already been snippy because Ben and I had refused to leave while she examined his injury. 'The Boss lady isn't going to turn up too, is she? Only we might need to borrow a bench from the cafeteria if she does and then they'll really hate us.'

'I don't think she turns up at hospitals. That means missions are failures usually,' Ben said.

'What do you mean, failures? We rescued Natalya. Well, to be honest, she had virtually rescued herself. If they'd had any nourishment on site she'd never have blacked out.' I'd left her the last of the snacks and water that I'd packed before we headed to the hospital. 'The entire gang has been arrested,' I pointed out.

'And Eli is here with a hole in his leg. It wasn't as under the radar as she was hoping.'

'Maybe she should have sent you in with enough back-up that they couldn't get the jump on you,' I suggested.

'Ben is right,' Eli chipped in, as he struggled to pull himself upright in bed. I moved to help him, but he waved me off. 'I can manage. Why don't you find us some chairs? They said I just need to wait for a prescription for some antibiotics then I can go, but the walk-in centre got closed last year and they're snowed under. I think I'm going to be a while. The Boss isn't going to show up. She'll be too busy working out who she's going to rip another hole in for letting one of those bozos get loose in the first place.'

'The answer is that you're all on my shit list,' the Boss lady said, as I swept open the cubicle curtain to find her stood there. 'Thankfully, despite the inept behaviour of your team which led to an entirely preventable injury and the potential issues our agency could face because you have accessed civilian healthcare with a gunshot wound, we seem to have everything in hand.'

'Eli has been shot!' I pointed out, rather loudly. Maybe a little too loudly, because my dad, who was stood next to me, tried to grab my arm, Erin covered her face with one hand and Ben turned away to face the wall to avoid the conflict. 'Okay, I'm going. I'll fetch extra chairs. But no-one gets told off before I get back to defend them.'

Chapter Forty-One

'Thank goodness they've gone and I've got you all to myself.' Eli leant forward on his bed and placed a kiss on my forehead.

'Don't get any ideas,' I warned him. 'These curtains might offer a semblance of privacy but it's an illusion. The guy next door just got given a suppository and I can't get my butt to unclench. The sound effects alone made me shake. Besides, our lot haven't gone far. Dad is trying to find something vaguely more nutritious than cardboard in the food hall, Cody decided that a few pictures of the hospital would be great for her exhibition so she's off trying to get consent from the staff to take a few shots.' I cringed after I said it. 'Bad choice of words, but you know what I mean. Ben heard a registrar complaining that the IT system was running slow, but they caught him using their desktop without permission. Luckily, he had finished fixing it and they're blown away by the improvement, but Erin is still busy trying to make sure that he doesn't get arrested. Again.'

Eli patted the space on the bed next to him, a good foot closer than I was currently sitting. 'Scoot up.' I didn't scoot. 'Are you angry with me?' he asked.

'No,' I said.

'The stress lines on your forehead beg to differ.'

I blew out a sigh. There was no easy way to break it to Eli that I hated his job. I understood why he did it, and I was grateful that there were people out there who were willing to risk their lives in order to keep the rest of us safe, but I hated that Eli had to be one of them. It had taken us years to get together. I didn't want to throw it away. If I asked him to choose between me and his job, I was pretty sure that he would choose me, but not certain. Plus, I didn't want to be that kind of person. I didn't want him to have to choose. His career was such an integral part of who he was: strong, protective and above all, loyal. Did I want to be selfish in the face of his selflessness?

Eli shifted himself further down towards me instead, grunting with the effort. He put his arm around me, and I rested my head against his shoulder. The hospital gown was soft under my cheek from the thousands of washes. It felt comforting to be held, but after a couple of deep breaths I sat up straight again.

'Ready to talk?' he asked.

'No,' I answered. 'Not really.'

Eli tucked a strand of hair behind my ear and kissed me again. Despite the dissonance in my brain, I found myself kissing him back. 'How about now?'

'I hate your job, but I don't want to stop you being true to yourself. You can ask me to stay away from your missions if you want to, because it's not my job and you hate me being in danger. I can't ask the same of you.'

'It's not as though you pay any attention when I do ask though, is it?' He entwined his fingers with mine. 'I should have given you more credit. Again. It was thanks to you that we found Natalya in time to save her. She was seriously dehydrated. Did you see how wobbly she was after she let go of you?'

'I was too busy rubbing my throat where she grabbed me. But she did down the first bottle of water I gave her. It was a good job there was another in my bag.'

'What I don't understand though is why you were running for the outhouse after you saw my injury? You're not squeamish. You used to patch me up all the time after me and Ben got into fights at school.'

'Ben never got into fights,' I pointed out. It had always been Eli who had needed cleaning up, his nose strapping up because it was bleeding after a punch, or a cold pack for a black eye.

'No, he caused enough though; correcting a teacher's grammar, lecturing all the kids behind the bike shed about how bad it is for your health to smoke.' Eli had stepped in to save him from all of those situations.

'Why did you hang out with us? It can't have been for the scintillating conversation. I only understand about half of what Ben says and I'm his twin.'

'Must have been because I fancied you.' He gave my shoulder a little nudge and I cracked a smile, so he nudged me again, and put his arm back around me as I laughed. 'Honestly, I liked that I always knew where I stood with him. He always told the truth, never played head games. I was a lonely kid, it was only me and my mum. When I stood up for him that first day at school, he glued himself to my side, and all of a sudden I had a best friend. Now, are you going to answer my question? Why were you running?'

'I thought I was going to throw up,' I told him. Suddenly the curtains opened and Lily's face poked round it.

'Uh oh, morning sickness alert,' she joked. 'What did I tell you about safe sex?'

'Enough to write several books which need to be kept on high shelves,' I told her. 'But I'm not pregnant.'

'No method of birth control is a hundred per cent safe. And I assume you guys have a pretty healthy sex life?'

'Healthier than yours,' Eli said, winking at her.

'I doubt it. I don't think you two have the stamina. Or the imagination.'

The curtains jerked open again, and Ben and Erin rejoined us. 'What's so funny?' Ben asked.

'We're wondering if Daisy is pregnant,' Lily informed him. 'She's been feeling nauseous.'

'My boyfriend had just been shot,' I pointed out. 'I'm not pregnant. Besides, if I was, don't you think that Eli would look a lot more nervous?' I gestured at said boyfriend, who was grinning, obviously proud at the notion of his virility being powerful enough to overcome even the most stringent birth control approach. 'I don't think we're ready for a life of fractured sleep and nappies.' Eli's grin began to fade. 'We were just talking about how we hate each other being in dangerous situations but we don't know what to do about it. There is no way we can have a baby right now.'

By the time I finished speaking Eli had fallen completely still, his eyes wide open and staring. He wasn't smiling anymore. 'When was your last ... you know?' he asked.

'My last period? You can say the words. They're not scary. Messy maybe, and uncomfortable definitely.' I got my phone out and began to count the days on my calendar. 'Twenty ... nine days.'

'Oh shit,' said Lily. Eli and I shared the sentiment.

'Do we need to get you a pregnancy test?' Erin asked. 'We are in a hospital.'

'We're in A&E, they're hardly going to want to take the time to deal with me.'

'If you're pregnant then it was an accident and I need to know as a matter of some emergency,' Eli said.

'I can hack into their system and sort out the paperwork for you, order you a test?' Ben offered.

'No!' Erin and I shouted at the same time.

Lily began to rummage through her handbag. 'Tissues, no ...' she handed them to Ben. 'Handcuffs.' She handed those to Erin who dropped them on the bed with a whimper and rubbed her hands on her skirt. Eventually Lily gave up digging and tipped the handbag out onto the bed, and there, hidden beneath a pile of lace and bottles and paddles and leather, was a little white box, just like the one I'd seen before our Paris trip. She handed it to me. 'I'd bought a twin pack just to be on the safe side, but I think you need this one more than I do. You just pee on the stick.'

'I don't need to go.'

Eli stood up, grimacing as he put some weight on his

injured leg. He poured me a glass of water from the plastic jug on his side table and handed it to me. 'Drink,' he commanded. I took the glass and downed it. He took the empty cup and refilled it. I downed that too. 'And now?' Lily asked.

'Give me a minute.'

Eli went to refill the glass, but I stopped him. 'I'm good to go.' Lily went to follow me out to the ladies' loo but Eli stopped her and followed me instead. The cubicles were full, but the corridors were empty. Still, I hissed at Eli 'What are you doing?'

'Coming with you. It's my baby.'

'There is no baby.'

'We'll see.'

On the corner, a couple of nurses were gathered, comparing notes. There was a large whiteboard with the cubicles and they were discussing the referrals, results and prescriptions that they were waiting on. As we hurried past, I glanced up at the wall. I shouldn't have been surprised not to see Eli's name on it. 'You checked in as Ian Fleming?'

He shrugged. As we reached the door to the toilets, Eli opened it for me. I walked in, and he followed. 'This is a ladies' toilet,' I pointed out.

'My love, you have been hanging around with Lily for so long I'm not sure that even you still qualify as a lady.'

I stuck my tongue out at him, ignoring the fact that I was being goaded by his teasing into confirming his aspersions, and shoved him back outside. Then I locked myself into a cubicle and peed on the stick.

Chapter Forty-Two

'Daisy, are you ready to go?' Dad shouted down the stairs to me. I finished brushing my hair, slipped on my heels and went up to join him. He was dressed in a black suit. The only concession he had made to his new, more colourful, persona was the rainbow-striped tie.

I straightened the knot, and noticed that he had a matching waistcoat too, mostly hidden beneath his jacket. I kissed his cheek, feeling the rough graze of his stubble. He'd even shaved for the event, although it felt as though he had shaved a day or two too early. 'How is Cody holding up?' I asked.

'She's pinging between nervous and excited every other minute. Or maybe she's nervously excited. Or excitedly nervous. Anyway, she changed her outfit five times, her shoes three and her hairstyle twice. If watching Lily and you getting ready over the years has taught me anything, it's that she may or may not be ready to leave on time.'

'You didn't say that to her, did you?'

'Most certainly not.' Dad chuckled. I still wasn't quite used to seeing him cheerful, and I grabbed my phone to take a quick photo. It wouldn't be up to the standard of the pictures that Cody would be displaying shortly but I wanted the memento nonetheless. 'I told her she looked beautiful in everything she showed me.'

'Dad, you're wonderful, but that probably didn't help her decide anything. You lock up here, I'll scoot across to her house quickly and help her finish up.' I kissed his cheek again, headed back down the stairs so that I could exit through my flat, and stopped for just long enough to grab a jewellery box from underneath the counter on my way out.

I crossed the cobbled path which separated Cody's home

and gallery from my own, admired the hanging basket by her front door and lifted the bronze knocker. The door swung open in my hand. I called out, hoping not to scare her. 'Cody, it's Daisy. Can I come in?'

'Back here. Can you give me a hand with this zip?' I followed the sounds of her voice, past the white walls of her studio, hung with the landscapes and close-ups of flora and fauna. She had used these images to reinvent herself following a breakdown. Cody had never shown us any of the pictures which she had taken before her illness, but I'd seen a couple when we were first finding out who she was. I wasn't surprised it had taken a toll on her mental health. She had seen hell on earth and been able to capture the details so that those of us in comparative safety could share the guilt, fear and pain. Sadly, the wars and natural disasters which had helped Cody to win international awards for her work continued, though Cody herself no longer witnessed their horrors.

I found the lady herself wearing a suit as smart as my dad's. It was just as dark and sombre, and Cody looked every bit the same. Her usually radiant smile was absent, and I missed it. She gestured to the zip on the back of her skirt. 'I haven't worn this since before.' I assumed she meant before the illness. 'You might need to hold the fabric together with one hand and then yank the zip. I think I've put some weight on recently. Your dad's cooking is too good to resist. And he makes me feel beautiful. I've stopped caring about the extra pound or two. Or ten.'

I pulled the zip, and though it didn't want to move at first, I eventually dragged it closed. 'You are beautiful,' I told her. 'Plus, you're the reason we have my dad back. I'll be forever grateful to you for that.' I handed her the jewellery box. 'This is a little something for you, to wish you all the best for today.'

Cody opened the box, gazed at the pendant inside, and

then drew me in for a hug. I breathed in the lavender and patchouli. Cody handed me back the leather string with the four-leaf clover encased in a drop of glass to fasten around her neck.

I apologised as I did so. 'I wanted to wish you luck, but this isn't nearly as smart as your outfit. Are you sure you want to wear it? I've got a necklace in my shop with a pearl and diamond pendant. Let me go and fetch that for you.'

Cody stopped me. 'This is the perfect necklace for today. If anything is wrong, it's my choice of outfit. Please can you unzip me again? I can't breathe in these clothes. And not because of your dad's pastries either. This isn't me anymore.' She slipped the jacket off, put it back on a hanger and placed it back inside her wardrobe. On her bed were a pile of brightly coloured fabrics. I couldn't tell the dresses from the skirts from the shawls by their shape. Cody knew exactly what she was after, though. She sorted through the fabrics until she found a lilac cotton shirt dress with silver edges. Underneath that she pulled on turquoise silk trousers. The final touch was a burnt orange silk scarf in her auburn hair. She looked striking, cheerful and utterly perfect.

'Thank you for coming into our lives and making my dad smile again,' I said.

'Thank you for welcoming me,' she replied. 'It must have been strange, when it had been just the three of you for so long.'

'There were four of us, mostly,' I told her, 'even when Eli and I were pretending that we couldn't stand each other, he was always there.'

'Have you spoken to him today?'

I shook my head. 'He's been staying back at his old flat sorting it out, but I'm sure he wouldn't miss this.' I'd text him once we got outside. Our communication had been somewhat strained since his hospital stay, but it was time to face up to it.

'Daisy.' Cody grew serious, taking my hands in hers and breathing deeply. I could see a flush on her already rosy cheeks. 'Do you think that your dad would ever get married again?'

I'd honestly never thought about it, and it took me a moment to get my head around the idea, but once I had, it seemed like a no-brainer. 'I think he might,' I told her. 'My mum was his childhood sweetheart. He'll never forget her, but I think he's finally ready to live for himself again too. I think he's ready to think about it, more than I ever thought he would be, though if you're asking if he's dropped any hints yet, he hasn't. He probably wanted to wait until he's sure that you're ready too, though I can have a word with him, if you'd like? Suss him out a bit?'

'Actually, I was thinking of asking him.' Despite me thinking of myself as a modern woman, it hadn't occurred to me that this might even be a possibility. 'Would you mind?' Cody asked. 'I'd only go ahead if it was alright with you and Ben. I don't want to do anything that would disrespect your mum.'

'I think she would be very grateful to you for bringing him back to life.'

Cody glowed. She held out her arms and I stepped into them. She gave me the sort of hug I had been missing for years. It was just what I needed, and I found myself crying. Cody let go of the hug but rested her hands gently on my shoulders. 'Are you okay?'

I nodded but couldn't bring myself to answer. 'We'd better go,' I said, in lieu of a proper response to her question. 'Dad's booked a taxi.'

'He's a thoughtful man,' Cody said, and it was true, but he had become more so since he had met her. 'It's not far by tube.'

'He thought we'd like to arrive without travelling like sardines.' I wiped away the tears, and together we headed off to the opening of Cody's exhibition.

Chapter Forty-Three

The exhibition was well attended, and I lost sight of my dad almost immediately amongst the crowds. I caught the occasional glimpse of Cody's hair and scarf above the heads of the other guests, but I couldn't get close enough to speak to her. She seemed to be surrounded at all times by people cooing and ahhing over pictures. As well they might. The images were as striking as any I had ever seen. Some captured views of the city I knew and loved, but portrayed it in ways that I had never seen before.

One showed the London Eye, which I remembered so well from our meeting with Jean-Luc, or Laurent, to give him his proper name. In Cody's image though, the enormous wheel was in the background, slightly out of focus because what had captured her attention, and now captivated mine, was the sight of two small children holding ice creams. The children's T-shirts were covered in drips where the sweet dessert had melted in the sun. The blond boy, aged maybe three at most, held out his strawberry, and the girl with her hair in the most beautiful of braids was holding a cone of mint choc-chip. They were leaning into each other and tasting each other's ice creams. I found my eyes filling with tears yet again, and I hurried to try and blink them away.

Waiters, dressed all in black but for their crisp white aprons, circulated carrying trays of sparkling wine and canapes. Eli appeared from behind a group of people admiring the pictures of a wedding party emerging from a church. He snagged two glasses from a passing waiter and handed one to me.

'How are you? I haven't seen you much since the hospital.'

I sipped the wine. 'Better now, thank you.' I drained the glass, handed it back to him, took his and drank that too.

'We need to talk,' he said.

'What's the point?' I looked around to see if I could score more drinks.

'Daisy, you were as relieved as I was when the test came back negative.'

'I was,' I said, 'and I told you it would. But what I didn't expect was to feel sad about it. I do want to have a baby, maybe not right now, but in the next couple of years perhaps. But how can I do that when you're terrified of me doing anything you consider slightly risky, but you put yourself in situations all the time for work where you get shot?'

'I've only been shot once,' Eli protested.

'Isn't that enough for you?' I managed to grab another glass of wine and looked around to find a quieter spot. There wasn't one, so I made for the balcony. The alcohol had brought a flush to my cheeks and the air outside was too warm to help it fade. Eli followed me, but he waited for me to be ready to speak again. 'How can we plan for a life together when we have lifestyles like this? And I can't ask you to give your job up. I won't. You love what you do, and the country is lucky to have you. I don't want to make you give up something which is intrinsic to who you are, but I'm not sure I can have children and not know whether you're going to be there to watch them grow up. I don't want them to suffer the grief and pain that we did.'

'They wouldn't' Eli assured me. 'They would be surrounded by love, from you, from Ben, from your dad , Cody, Lily and Erin. Besides, no-one can guarantee that they won't get ill or have an accident. Life doesn't work that way.'

'Eli, I can't imagine my life without you, but I don't know how to resolve this.'

Eli glanced around the balcony and spotted a couple of old wrought iron chairs. They must have weighed a ton, but he lifted them easily and carried them over so that we could sit down. Closing the glass doors behind us, the hum from the crowds inside was silenced. I looked out over the River Thames, watching the ripples from so high above that they were hardly visible amongst the grey murky water.

'I love this city, and I promised that I would do anything to keep it safe, but I don't want to lose you to do it.' He rubbed his face with both hands, and the armour of elegance and sophistication that he usually wore slipped, just a little. 'Do you remember when Ben made us watch the *Star Trek* film, the one where they talk about Captain Kirk being the only cadet to ever pass the unpassable test? The only person to find a solution to a question that was never designed to be solved, but to see how cadets responded in that situation?'

'The Kobayashi Maru. I remember.'

'We had something similar, Taylor and I, when we were being trained. We had to choose whether to most likely sacrifice ourselves and stay to try to deactivate a bomb that was hidden in a school. It was that or try and evacuate, but with only a few seconds left on the clock it wouldn't be long enough to get many people out.'

'What did you do?'

'I started cutting wires at random just in case it worked and waited to be blown to hell. We didn't know it was a decoy set to test us. I thought I was going to die. But I knew that it was that, or risk leaving hundreds of kids to die. I'd never have saved them all any other way. There wasn't time.'

'And Taylor?'

'Ran. He claimed he was trying to give the order to evacuate as he ran, but the Boss told him later that he was just screaming. Oh, he might have survived, with a few others who copied him, but a bunch of kids wouldn't have. After that he always thought I was too impulsive, too quick to risk my life and that of anyone who was with me.'

'And you thought that he was a coward who wouldn't take the hard decisions. No wonder you hated each other.'

'We did,' Eli agreed, loosening his tie and unbuttoning the

top of his shirt to try in vain to cool down. 'But we don't any more. Taylor risked his life coming with me to the barn.'

'But does he still think that you're impulsive? Bordering on suicidal?'

'I'm not,' Eli assured me, taking my hand in his. 'I've got far too much to live for. And this isn't *Star Trek*. My job isn't the Kobayashi Maru. My job isn't unwinnable. There are risks, but they're usually carefully assessed.'

'Too bad you're not still channelling your inner Captain Kirk,' I told him, getting up to sit on his knee and thread my fingers through his hair. 'Lily just texted me to say that she had one of those short *Star Trek* uniform dresses in stock. I thought it might be rather fun.'

'I want to have fun,' Eli said, trailing feather kisses down my neck, 'but I want more too. I want us, Daisy, forever.'

'So do I,' I told him.

'The Boss was very impressed by your bravery, and your ability to throw the chain on target under pressure. She somehow got a copy of your aptitude test, the one you took to get Ben to come along and take it too.'

'How did she get that? Ben?'

Eli shook his head. 'Me. I was wrong, Daisy, so wrong. I'm sorry. It's actually safer having you help me after all. I reckon there might be a job going if you want it?'

'Could I fit it around my work at the shop?'

'Might be worth a try,' Eli suggested. 'Maybe we'd feel safer if we were at work together?'

'Does that mean I can count you in for a few shifts selling frilly knickers?' I teased.

'I'll do anything to make you happy, Daisy,' he said. Eli began to reach into his pocket, but from behind us, a round of applause and cheering broke out so loudly that we could hear it through the closed doors. We got up and opened them, poking our heads into the room, and spotted my dad and Cody being toasted. They wore matching silver bands on their left hands. We waved and blew them kisses, but once they were distracted again by the crowds of well-wishers we returned to our seat outside. 'I think your dad's news goes hand in hand with mine,' Eli continued. 'Ben told me he was thinking of moving in with Erin, and it looks like your dad won't be moving back from Cody's after all. I asked him earlier if I could stay, and he suggested we take over the rest of the house, move upstairs, make it a home. There's space for us each to have more than a couple of drawers. What do you say?' Eli took my hand and placed a keyring into it. It was the shape of half a heart. In his hand was the other half, complete with a key to my house. 'Shall we? Let's live together properly, find a path where we can do what we love without fear of hurting or losing each other?'

I threw my arms around him and kissed him. 'That sounds perfect to me.'

Thank You

Dear Reader,

Thank you for reading *Daisy's Summer Mission*. I wasn't ready to let go of the characters after writing about their first adventures in *Daisy's Christmas Gift Shop*. I wanted to see what mischief Daisy and Lily got up to next and I hope you enjoyed finding out too!

I would like to thank the Choc Lit family for their continued support. Thanks too, to the Choc Lit taster panel for taking a chance on my books. I'm so excited to be on this journey with such a welcoming and lovely group of people.

If you have enjoyed reading this story it would mean a lot to me if you had a few minutes to share a review.

Love Hannah

x

About the Author

Hannah Pearl was born in East London. She is married with two children and now lives in Cambridge.

She has previously worked as a Criminology researcher at a university in Leicester, as a Development Worker with various charities and even pulled a few pints in her time.

In 2015 she was struck down by Labrynthitis, which left her feeling dizzy and virtually housebound. She has since been diagnosed with ME. Reading has allowed Hannah to escape from the reality of feeling ill. She read upwards of three hundred books during the first year of her illness. When her burgeoning eReader addiction grew to be too expensive, she decided to have a go at writing. In 2017 she won Simon & Schuster's Books and the City #heatseeker short story competition, in partnership with *Heat* magazine, for her short story *The Last Good Day*.

Hannah is a member of the Romantic Novelists Association.

Follow Hannah:
www.dizzygirlwrites.wordpress.com
Twitter: www.twitter.com/HannahPearl_1

More Ruby Fiction

From Hannah Pearl

Daisy's Christmas Gift Shop

Struggling to find the perfect Christmas gift? Step into Romantic Daze ...

Daisy Kirk is a sucker for a love story, which is why she opened up her gift shop – because there's nothing that makes Daisy happier than when she's helped a customer achieve their own 'happily ever after' by finding the perfect Christmas gift for their loved one. And she absolutely does not just sell 'soppy presents and frilly pants' as her brother's infuriating best friend, Eli, is so fond of suggesting.

The sad fact is that whilst Daisy is helping others with their love lives, hers is non-existent. But when unusual circumstances take Daisy and Eli on a road trip from London to rural Wales, will she finally get the happily ever after to her own Christmas love story?

Visit www.rubyfiction.com for details.

Evie's Little Black Book

Is hunting down every man you've kissed the answer to finding Mr Right?

When Evie is invited to the wedding of the guy she'd fancied throughout her teens, it's the final straw. What's wrong with her and why can't *she* keep a man?

In between consoling herself with ice cream and chocolate, and sobbing her heart out to her cousin Charmaine, Evie has a brainwave – and it all centres around her 'little black book' (well, more floral patterned notebook really) – which contains the details of every man she's ever kissed or dated. Perhaps the cure for her disastrous love life has been nestled within its pages all along …

Does Evie's little black book really hold the answers, or will learn she learn that exes are exes for a reason?

Visit www.rubyfiction.com for details.

It's My Birthday

Oh boy, another birthday …

Karen could be excused for crying on her birthday, especially as it's the first one since her husband got on a plane to the States and never came back. Then there's the fact that her workmates were practically bribed to attend her birthday meal. But when a restaurant double booking leads to her sharing a table with single dad Elliot and his daughter, things start looking up.

As Karen gets to know Elliot she experiences feelings she thought she'd never have again. But is it enough? Or will the thing that destroyed Karen's previous relationship also ruin things with Elliot?

Visit www.rubyfiction.com for details.